BOARDING SCHOOL MYSTERIES

SMOKE SCREEN

Other books in the growing Faithgirlz!™ Library

Boarding School Mysteries
Fading Tracks (Book One)
Secrets for Sale (Book Two)
Pick Your Poison (Book Four)

The Sophie series
Sophie's World (Book One)
Sophie's Secret (Book Two)
Sophie and the Scoundrels (Book Three)
Sophie's Irish Showdown (Book Four)
Sophie's First Dance? (Book Five)
Sophie's Stormy Summer (Book Six)
Sophie Breaks the Code (Book Seven)
Sophie Tracks a Thief (Book Eight)
Sophie Flakes Out (Book Nine)
Sophie Loves Jimmy (Book Ten)
Sophie Loses the Lead (Book Eleven)
Sophie's Encore (Book Twelve)

The Blog On series
Grace Notes (Book One)
Love, Annie (Book Two)
Just Jazz (Book Three)
Storm Rising (Book Four)
Grace Under Pressure (Book Five)
Upsetting Annie (Book Six)
Jazz Off-Key (Book Seven)
Storm Warning (Book Eight)

Other books by Kristi Holl
What's A Girl to Do?
Shine on, Girl!: Devotions to Keep You Sparkling
Girlz Rock: Devotions for You
Chick Chat: More Devotions for Girls
No Boys Allowed: Devotions for Girls

Check out www.faithgirlz.com

faThGirLz!
2 corinthians 4:18

BOARDING SCHOOL MYSTERIES
SMOKE SCREEN

KRISTI HOLL

ZONDERkidz

ZONDERVAN.com/
AUTHORTRACKER
follow your favorite authors

Smoke Screen
Copyright © 2008 by Kristi Holl
Illustrations © 2008 by Bruce Emmett

Requests for information should be addressed to:
Zonderkidz, *Grand Rapids, Michigan* 49530

Library of Congress Cataloging-in-Publication Data

Holl, Kristi.
    Smoke Screen /by Kristi Holl.
        p. cm. -- (Faithgirlz) (Boarding school mysteries ; bk. 3)
        ISBN 978-0-310-71431-6 (softcover)
      [1. Boarding schools--Fiction. 2. Schools--Fiction. 3. Arson--Fiction.
    4. Christian life--Fiction. 5. Mystery and detective stories.] I. Title.
    PZ7.H7079Sm 2008
    [Fic]--dc22
                                       2008008349

Editor: Barbara Scott
Art direction & cover design: Sarah Molegraaf
Interior design: Carlos Eluterio Estrada

Printed in the United States of America

08 09 10 11 12 • 5 4 3 2 1

So we fix our eyes not on what is seen, but what is unseen.
For what is seen is temporary, but what is unseen is eternal.

— 2 Corinthians 4:18

TABLE OF CONTENTS

1

ALARM!

Today was a day for wrapping up in a warm blanket with hot chocolate—not trudging through depressing drizzle to Thursday's biology lab. "Rain, rain, go away," Jeri McKane chanted, "but *don't* come again another day." She pulled open the door to Herald Hall.

Abby Wright, in her matching blue school uniform, sprayed droplets as she shook her pink umbrella. "But April showers bring May flowers, right?"

"So far only April mud." Jeri plodded up the creaking wooden stairs after Abby, yawning as they reached the third floor.

Near their lab, a fifteen-year-old boy was mopping, dragging his bucket on wheels behind him. Jeri watched three sixth-grade girls pass by. One kicked his bucket,

7

and another knocked off his baseball cap. The third girl laughed and said, "Think you can handle the job, retard?" before ducking into the lab.

Jeri clenched her jaw. Why do special needs kids get picked on all the time? Just because they have learning problems doesn't mean they have no feelings!

Tim stooped to grab his cap. Arms waving wildly, he slipped on the wet floor and fell hard on one knee.

Jeri hurried to give him a hand up. "Just ignore them," she said, flipping her straight brown hair over her shoulder.

"It's okay." Overweight and pockmarked with acne, Tim Norton towered above her. "I don't mind."

Through a jobs program for special needs students, Tim and three other teens worked mornings at the girls' boarding school. In the afternoons they attended classes at the New Hope Academy, a school in Landmark Hills for those with mental disabilities.

"You okay, Tim?" Abby asked, her light blonde eyebrows raised in concern. "Those beastly girls are so blinkered."

Jeri nodded, totally agreeing with the British word for narrow-minded.

"They just like to tease me." Tim blushed and then held out his cap. "Wanna see something new?" His ball cap was covered with colorful buttons with sayings like "Hollyweird" and "Future Movie Star." He pointed to a smiling strawberry button called "Merry Berry." Another one showed a dolphin with a club called "Golphin' Dolphin."

"Awesome buttons," Jeri said, turning the cap around and around to read them.

Abby touched Jeri's arm. "I need to measure our bean plant before class. Maybe that Miracle-Gro did its magic over the weekend."

Jeri grinned. "Yeah. Hopefully it looks like the one in 'Jack and the Beanstalk.'"

"No! Jeri and the Beanstalk!" Tim laughed so hard at his own joke that his eyes watered.

With posture fit for the queen of England, Abby glided down the hall and disappeared into the science room. Because the lab was so small, only eight students were scheduled at a time.

Tim pushed his mop in a circle, the gray strings smearing more than cleaning the mud. "Somebody made tracks all over. I'm cleaning it up."

"Sorry we're so sloppy."

"But I like to mop! I like rain too. It makes the grass grow." Tim stood taller and grinned. "Mr. Rankin said I can clean the lawn mowers this week." He puffed out his chest. "I like Mr. Rankin."

Jeri tucked her lower lip in. Personally, she thought the loud, droopy-eyed groundskeeper at the boarding school wasn't much friendlier than a snake. But if Tim liked working for him, great. She stuck Tim's cap on her own dark hair. He swiped at it several times, but Jeri ducked out of reach.

Two girls passed them. One whispered, "You two make such a cute couple." The girls dissolved in laughter. "A match made in heaven," the other one said.

Jeri's face grew warm. Normally she wasn't bothered by what people thought about her, but those girls' teasing bugged her. She was suddenly embarrassed about befriending Tim—but why? Why care what they thought now?

She handed back his cap, waved, and followed the girls to the science room. Something wispy caught her eye, and she glanced up. Gauzy gray strands floated out the transom window above the door. *Was that smoke?*

Before she could decide, an explosion blasted her eardrums. The heavy wooden door rattled on its hinges. Glass from the transom shattered, raining down like sleet. Several shards skittered across the black-and-white tile and hit Jeri's feet.

"Fire!" someone screamed in the lab. Simultaneously, the fire alarm sounded. The clanging was deafening. *Abby!* She had to find her! Was she hurt? Tim clutched her arm, but Jeri peeled him off. He covered his ears and twisted side to side.

Smoke poured into the hall. Five or six students ran from the room, coughing and choking. Their biology teacher, Ms. Todd, sprang from her office next door and raced to the lab. She herded the coughing students to the exit at the other end of the hall.

Jeri pressed back against the wall, out of the flow of traffic. Next to her, Tim rolled his eyes while rubbing his knuckles against his mouth. Jeri squinted through the smoke and peered into the lab, hunting for Abby. *Where is she?* Overhead sprinklers were spraying the room, soaking books and papers. "Abby!" she called, her eyes stinging.

Within seconds, Lyndsey Powers staggered out, tears streaming down her flushed face that was streaked with black. Her short brown hair was plastered to her head, making her brown eyes look enormous.

"Don't worry," she said, gasping. "I'm the last one out."

"No, you're not," Jeri said. "I haven't seen Abby!" She started into the room.

A hand grabbed her. "Don't go in there!" Ms. Todd ordered, her slender fingers digging into Jeri's arm.

"But Abby—"

"*Stay here.*" The teacher entered the smoky lab, and Jeri watched her search the small room. Despite the sprinklers, the fire had spread from the metal wastebasket by the window and was consuming everything on the teacher's desk. Dashing to her file cabinet, Ms. Todd knelt down and helped Abby up from the floor. Supporting her around the waist, they stumbled from the lab, coughing. Both were dripping from the sprinklers. Jeri put her arm around Abby's other side.

Suddenly Lyndsey pushed Tim aside and wheeled his sloshing bucket of water into the science lab.

"Come back!" Jeri shouted.

Lyndsey ignored her and rolled the bucket across the lab's tile floor. She hoisted the bucket in her arms and dumped some of the water in the trash can. A long hiss was followed by more smoke billowing out the door. She poured the rest on Ms. Todd's burning desk.

Jeri turned from the smoke in time to see Abby and Tim going down the stairs together. *Good.* Covering her mouth and nose, Jeri stepped just inside the lab.

Two windows were blown out, helping the smoke to clear. The fire was extinguished, thanks to Lyndsey's quick thinking, but the overhead sprinklers continued to rain in the lab. Student experiments and papers were soggy, the microscopes were wet, and water dripped from the skull of a life-sized skeleton hanging on a hook.

Ms. Todd dashed past Jeri and ushered Lyndsey out. "What were you *thinking*?" the teacher demanded.

A trickle of blood ran down Lyndsey's arm, but she didn't seem to notice. "I was feeding my minnows when there was this *boom*," she said, her voice hoarse. "Glass flew everywhere, and your papers were on fire."

"The fire's out now," Ms. Todd said, "but you should *never* have run back in there." The teacher's freckles stood out distinctly against her milky-white skin. "Leave firefighting to the firemen!"

Sirens wailed in the distance as Jeri followed Lyndsey and Ms. Todd down the stairs. She felt sorry for Lyndsey, getting chewed out by their teacher. She'd put the fire out way faster than those dinky sprinklers, and the building could have burned down before the firefighters got there.

Jeri stopped at the second floor landing. "Oh no. I forgot my backpack." She ran upstairs, grabbed it, and hurried down and outside. Ms. Todd and Lyndsey were already swallowed up by the crowd evacuated from Herald House.

Ms. Long, the headmistress, stood on the building's steps. Raindrops spotted her gray suit as she shouted into a bullhorn. "Clear the drive for emergency vehicles!" Her half-glasses swung on a chain around her neck. "Students! Move immediately!"

Jeri slipped around her and searched the crowd. *Where was Abby? Was she all right? What a morning!* At least the rain had stopped, although a fine mist shrouded the campus in fog. Finally she spotted Tim's bright orange jacket and head sticking above the crowd. She squinted. Was Abby with him? She couldn't tell. Jeri weaved toward him through small clusters of students.

He was in an earnest conversation with a seventh grader, Lisa Poole. "But I *want* you to wear it," Tim said, holding her arm. "It's my favorite button." In his palm was a pin with a kitty on it.

"I don't want your dumb pin. Let go before somebody sees you," Lisa hissed. She glanced at Jeri and then dismissed her with a beady-eyed look.

"But I bought this pin for you."

Lisa shook her streaked hair, making her dangling turquoise earrings dance. "What if I buy *you* a new pin instead?"

"Really?" Tim's face lit up.

"Yup, it's perfect for you. It has a brain walking on crutches." She snorted. "Get it? A lame brain." She smirked as she moved away.

Tim laughed too, but Jeri knew he'd just been insulted, even if he didn't get it. Mean people like Lisa really fried Jeri.

But Tim's attention was already on two yellow fire trucks and a police car rolling up the hill to the school. "Look, Jeri, just like TV! It's a pumper tanker and a ladder truck."

Jeri scanned the area, worried about her friend. "Did Abby go back to the dorm?"

"A teacher took her to the firmry."

Jeri blinked, hoping she'd misunderstood. "The *infirmary*?"

"I didn't have to go." Tim pounded his chest like Tarzan. "I'm too strong."

Jeri grabbed Tim's jacket sleeve. "Listen to me! Did Abby get burned? Was she cut by flying glass?" Jeri gave up. Racing around puddles and slipping on wet grass, she headed to Clarke Hall, which housed the student hospital. At the desk in the waiting room, she asked the elderly nurse about Abby.

"Yes, she's here, but what about your own cough, dear?" The plump, gray-haired nurse stood. "Were you near the fire, hon?"

"Yeah, but I'm fine."

"Let's get you an oxygen mask. You're short of breath."

"I was running, that's all," Jeri said. "I don't need oxygen."

"Dear, I'll be the judge of that. Is your saliva black or gray?" The nurse's double chin quivered. "Spit into this tissue for me."

Gross. "I don't need to. *Really.* I was only in the hall when it happened."

The nurse held out the tissue and waited, and Jeri spit. Her saliva was clear. After the nurse used a tongue depressor to peer down her throat, she used a tiny light to look up her nose. "No sign of burns. Good." The nurse held out a bottle of water in a veined hand. "Here."

After drinking some bottled water, Jeri pointed down the hall. "Can I see my friend now?"

"For just a minute. Her ambulance should arrive soon."

"*Ambulance?*" Jeri's voice squeaked. "Why?"

"Don't worry, it's just a precaution." The nurse patted Jeri's back. "She can't seem to stop coughing. I think she needs a bronchodilator."

"A what?"

"Something to relax the muscles in the respiratory system."

"Can't you give it to her here?"

"No, honey. They want to administer it along with a hospital procedure, called a bronchoscopy. A doctor uses a bronchoscope to look into her airways and lungs." At Jeri's puzzled look, she added, "It's a long thin tube with a light and camera on the end that goes down her throat."

Oh, gag, Jeri thought.

"We need to be careful," the nurse said. "Smoke can cause burns, as well as toxins in the blood stream, and lung damage. Your friend seems to have inhaled a lot of smoke."

"Can I stay with her until the ambulance comes? I know she'd want me to."

Jeri was pointed down the hall. Through two sets of double glass doors, she found a large room with half a dozen beds—all full. The tile floor squeaked with each step she took, and the room reeked of rubbing alcohol. Sliding curtains, hung to provide privacy around each bed, were pulled back.

Jeri had never seen the infirmary, but it had been a big selling point to her mom. Landmark School's catalogue had promised two nurses in residence, several hospital beds, and ambulance service to a hospital close by.

Jeri scanned the room, looking for the source of the coughing. Most of the patients were from Jeri's biology lab, and one was on oxygen. The three girls who'd made fun of Tim were there. So was Yolanda, a heavy-set girl with a sullen face who lived in Jeri's dorm. Jeri made a beeline for Abby, who was in the bed by the back window and bent over coughing.

"Halt!"

Jeri jumped, turning to find a middle-aged nurse behind her. Her bulbous nose was so round it looked fake, and bushy red eyebrows met over her nose. Her close-cropped, frizzled red hair completed her clown-like appearance. She was lean as a marathon runner, and sported an expensive brand of running shoes.

"I'm here to see my friend, uh ..." Jeri read the name badge. "Nurse Montgomery."

"No visitors. Zero." Her right hand sliced through the air.

Jeri took a deep breath. "The nurse out front said I could come back."

Nurse Montgomery pressed her lips into such a thin line that they disappeared. "Five minutes then. This is a hospital." She turned to the chattering girls and raised her voice. "Quiet in here!"

Jeri tiptoed over to Abby. The head of the bed was raised, and Abby lay propped up on two pillows. "How are you?" Jeri whispered.

Abby hacked and coughed, holding her stomach. "I feel like honking," she said, her voice hoarse.

"You need something to throw up in?"

"Nah, I've got that." She pointed to a turquoise plastic container on a rolling cart by her bed.

Abby had been sick all last week with a nasty virus, and she already looked awfully frail to Jeri. Perching on the edge of her bed, Jeri reached for a blue blanket to cover Abby's thin legs.

"Visitors do *not* sit on the beds!" the nurse snapped.

Jeri jumped up. "Sorry," she muttered. She leaned near Abby. "The other nurse said you're going to the hospital."

Abby nodded and blinked red, irritated eyes. "Breathed in too much smoke, I guess." She coughed again, so long her face turned a deep purple. "My head really hurts."

"Where were you at the time of the explosion?"

"By the teacher's desk. I was leaving our folder and measurements for her."

As Jeri patted Abby's back, feeling helpless, two young men pushed through the double doors and headed their way, rolling a skinny bed on wheels. "Hello, young lady," the short, stout one said. "Heard you've taken up smoking!"

Abby smiled at his feeble joke and then bent double, coughing again. Jeri moved out of the way so he could take her pulse and listen to her chest with a stethoscope. "Pulse is a bit slow," he said, "but your lungs sound normal. Excellent." He helped Abby crawl up onto the stretcher and covered her with a white knit blanket.

"When will she be back?" Jeri asked.

"Don't know. Depends on her tests."

"Can I come with her?"

"Sorry." He shook his head. "No."

Jeri picked up Abby's pink-and-purple backpack. "I'll put this in your room." If only she could go along! "Get better. We still have to practice the limbo dance for the luau."

Abby rolled on her side and curled up. "Right now I'd

rather have a kip in front of the telly than practice bending over backwards," she said with a wan smile.

"I hear ya." A nap in front of TV sounded good to Jeri too.

Hands clenched, she stepped back as they rolled Abby away. Her friend made a very small lump under the blanket. She could hear Abby coughing all the way down the hall.

2
ARSON

Jeri chewed her thumbnail, wishing she could go to the hospital with Abby. If only they'd let her ride along in the ambulance! Abby shouldn't be alone. *God, please make Abby better. Help her not to be afraid.*

In the bed beside her, Lyndsey removed her oxygen mask and laid it on her blanket. "She'll be okay," she said, her voice sympathetic. "The nurse said it wasn't serious."

"Maybe, but it's serious enough to go to the hospital." Jeri hung her head and took a deep breath. "Abby just got over the flu, and she's still weak."

Lyndsey ran fingers through her short hair, making it stand on end. "Man, that was some explosion."

"No joke. It even knocked out a couple windows."

"I bet it broke the fish tank and killed my minnows too," Lyndsey said.

"Might have." Jeri kept an eye out for Nurse Hitler. "How's your arm?"

"No stitches, the nurse said." Lyndsey held a three-inch square of white gauze in place. "Got cut by flying glass."

Hmmm, there's a story here, Jeri thought. *"Heroine Injured Saving Burning Building!"* Jeri immediately felt guilty. How could she think of that now? Still ... someone would report on the fire. Maybe she'd do it first. How awesome if she could scoop the *Lightning Bolt* senior editor with this story!

"What happened exactly?" Jeri asked, pulling her notebook from her backpack.

"I don't really know." Lyndsey rubbed her forehead. "I wasn't facing the teacher's desk." She cradled her sore arm protectively. "I was feeding my minnows, and suddenly, behind me there was this *boom*." She shuddered. "Fire was shooting out of the waste can, and the stuff on the desk was burning. I was afraid it would spread." A shadow passed over her face, and her fingers plucked nervously at the blanket.

"Putting the fire out with the bucket was fast thinking," Jeri said.

"Not really. A fast thinker would have remembered the fire extinguisher hanging on the wall."

Jeri scribbled fast, wishing she had a digital camera. A photo of Lyndsey, bandaged up in the hospital bed, would be a great touch. "You're a hero, you know."

"Ms. Todd didn't think so." Lyndsey's fingers were gripped together in her lap. "She yelled at me."

"She was scared you'd get hurt, that's all." Jeri hesitated and then asked, "If I check out a camera from the media lab, can I come back and take your picture?"

Lyndsey blinked. "What for?" She pushed her bangs out of her eyes, revealing an oddly-shaped pink birthmark.

Jeri tapped her pen on her notebook. "I write about French Club and Spanish Club for the *Lightning Bolt*, but I also put out a little sixth-grade newspaper." She explained that it was a media project she'd started last fall—a two-page newspaper mostly for her friends. Jeri's roommate, Rosa Sanchez, answered questions in her advice column. Abby covered music and art, and Abby's roommate, Nikki Brown, handled sports subjects. Jeri wrote the main features and edited everything. "I'd love to put you on the front page, if that's okay."

Lyndsey frowned. "Won't Ms. Todd get even madder?"

"Naw. Now that it's over, I bet she's glad you moved so fast. You saved nearly everything in the classroom."

"Well ..." Lyndsey finally smiled. "Sure. Why not?"

Jeri asked a few more questions about Lyndsey's family and hometown, discovering that she had a younger sister and came from Tampa, Florida.

Out of the corner of her eye, Jeri saw the red-haired nurse practically jogging from bed to bed on her Nike Airs. When she got to Lyndsey, Jeri felt a tap on her shoulder.

"You. Out!" She crossed her arms, her eyes unblinking. Then she turned to Lyndsey. "I need to dress your cut now." She removed the blanket and reached to pull the curtain around her bed. "Let's get you out of those wet clothes too."

"I'm not wet."

"Your tights are wet, and your jumper's damp. I'll have your house mother bring you some jeans or sweats."

"No, I'm fine!"

"We'll see about that." The nurse whipped the curtain closed around the bed.

Jeri wished she could change out of her own uniform. It wasn't wet, but she smelled like smoke. She pulled a strand of hair under her nose and sniffed. *El stinko.* It wasn't a nice campfire smoke smell. It had a bitter, metallic odor.

As Jeri left the infirmary, dime-sized drops of rain fell more heavily around her. A teacher holding a newspaper over her head ran across the glistening pavement. Across campus at Herald House, a small crowd was still gathered, with clumps of umbrellas looking like colorful mushrooms.

Two firefighters came out of the classroom building, talking and pointing, then moved to the side of the building. A three-part ladder extended from a fire truck like a tele-scope. The top of the ladder rested outside the science room window—or what was left of it. Jeri couldn't help wishing a rescue was in progress right this minute. What a photo op *that* would be!

Maybe she could still get a good quote for her article. If the school paper didn't want it, she could turn out a special edition of her own tonight and scoop them on the fire.

She spotted Tim hanging around a second fire truck, talking to its driver, and she headed that way. Waving his arms, Tim wielded his mop like a sword. Jeri hung back under a maple tree, waiting for him to finish.

"... and it was *my* water that put out the fire!" Tim said, making a comical salute.

"You carried the bucket to the third floor?" the firefighter asked. "That takes muscles."

"No. Mr. Rankin—he's my boss—took it on the elevator. I can't run the elevator." He studied his cap. "Hey, I lost something in there. Can I go back in?"

"Not till they finish their investigation, son." The firefighter stepped down from the truck and removed his bright yellow coat, revealing wide orange suspenders.

"Can I see your hood then?" Tim asked.

"Sure." The firefighter reached into the cab for it. "It's called a Nomex hood. See? This is a regulator hose." He slipped it on and adjusted it. "When it's worn correctly, it protects my head but doesn't limit my vision."

"Cool!" Tim touched the hood. "Want me to wash your truck for you?" He waved the mop strings in the firefighter's darkly tanned face.

Jeri cringed. Tim's behavior could be so embarrassing. She jerked as a cold drop of water hit her neck. She looked up. Rain was beginning to drip through the new spring leaves.

Shivering, Jeri was ready to head back to her dorm until she heard voices at the rear of the truck. One voice belonged to the headmistress. Jeri crept closer by inches, staying out of sight by the tanker and toolboxes while trying to hear.

A deep voice spoke. "Science labs are common scenes of accidental fires."

"Can you tell what happened?" Ms. Long asked.

Jeri inched closer, pencil poised. She might get her quote without having to ask any questions.

"I've been fire marshal for eighteen years," he said. "I always suspect dimwitted kids of being careless and combining combustible materials."

Jeri bristled at his tone. *Of all the nerve!*

"Excuse me, but our girls are *not* dimwitted." The Head's voice was icy. "Accidents happen."

"Look, lady, I only said I *suspected* carelessness."

Jeri's eyes bulged. *Nobody* called The Head *lady*! She leaned against the cold truck, straining to hear over Tim's chatter.

The fire marshal cleared his throat noisily. "After inspecting the scene and point of origin, I came to a different conclusion. It wasn't carelessness."

The Head's words were sharply clipped. "Then what started the fire?"

"Arson," he said. "That fire was set on purpose."

Jeri gasped at his words. Set on purpose? That wasn't possible ... was it? Who would do such a thing?

Images flashed through her mind: Smoke pouring from the room, students running for safety, Tim frozen in fear, Lyndsey's cut arm, and Abby being wheeled away on a stretcher. Someone caused that—not by accident—but *deliberately?*

Jeri shivered suddenly and violently. The idea of arson made her feel sick to her stomach. What friend or class-mate was really an enemy in disguise? She glanced up at the biology lab on the top floor of Herald Hall. Her whole class might have been trapped up there by flames—or forced to jump from third-story windows! *Abby and I could have been killed!*

Head Long finally found her voice. "Arson? Do you mean terrorism?" Her voice took on a deadly tone. "Or burning down a school building for the insurance money?"

"You can rule out terrorists." The fire marshal coughed. "Often insurance fraud *is* at the bottom of burning public buildings. I don't think so this time though."

"How was the fire started exactly? Matches? What?"

He was silent a moment. "This. A cheap disposable lighter. You can buy them anywhere. I found it smashed and floating in the water in the trash can."

"You must be wrong." The Head's voice was low, and Jeri strained to hear her words. "Ms. Todd said there was an explosion before the fire."

"Are you trying to tell me my job?" He cleared his throat, but it sounded like a growl. "These lighters will explode if left burning long enough. I had a case once where a boy watched the flame of his disposable lighter until it overheated, causing a small explosion." He shuffled his feet. "It ignited his clothing, and the boy died later from burns."

"You think that is what happened here?" The Head asked.

"No. I believe the lighter was used to set fire to some paper towels, and then some flammable liquid was added. A lab always contains flammable liquids. Could have been a cleaning solvent of some kind. I doubt your arsonist knew the lighter could explode when the liquid was added."

"Thank heavens no one's clothes caught fire!" The Head said.

"But my friends got hurt!" Jeri popped around the end of the fire truck, bumping into the fire marshal's back. "I overheard you," she explained. "My friend got cut, and Abby just went to the hospital for some doctor to stick a camera down her throat."

The fire marshal rocked back and forth. "I'm sorry to hear about your friends." His eyes were the bluest Jeri'd ever seen. "I'm just glad no one was killed."

"We could have been," Jeri said. "Which girl would do something like this? That is so sick!"

The fire marshal sat on the bumper of the fire truck, pulled on his earlobe, and then looked Jeri in the eye. "It's probably not a student. Arsonists usually set fires and then leave the immediate scene to escape being hurt."

"Then who?" Jeri asked.

"Lots of people were around—teachers, janitors, security, even strangers. This fire was apparently set just before class started. Not much damage occurred compared to what would have happened if the fire had been set after classes or in the night."

Jeri frowned. "Then what was the point?"

He pulled his earlobe again. "It could have been set to scare someone. We won't know until we've conducted a thorough investigation."

The Head touched Jeri's arm. "Second period is nearly half over already. You need to make it to your third-period class."

"All right."

Jeri looked up at the clock tower. She had thirty-five minutes. She ran to Hampton House, dropped Abby's backpack in her room, changed into her last clean jumper uniform, and headed back to the media lab to check out a digital camera. If she hurried, she could get Lyndsey's photo and still make it to class on time.

When she passed Herald Hall again, the sun was trying to break through the clouds, and the drizzle was ending. Firefighters had finished rolling up the hose and taken down the extension ladder. Tim was nowhere to be seen, but Jeri spotted Ms. Todd.

I should interview her too, she thought. But Ms. Todd looked exhausted. Covered with soot, she was deep in conversation with a security guard just outside the door. She'd catch her later, after getting the photo.

Back at the infirmary, Jeri hated seeing Abby's empty bed next to Lyndsey's. Three other beds besides Abby's were also stripped. Jeri tiptoed to the bed across the large room, keeping an eye peeled for Nurse Hitler. "How's your arm?" she asked.

"Not bad. It stung when she cleaned it out." Lyndsey grimaced. "Germs wouldn't dare to live with that nurse around."

Jeri laughed. "I got a camera. Can I take your picture now?" At her nod, Jeri positioned Lyndsey to show her bandaged arm better. "Smile, but not too much. A brave smile that shows you're in pain." She shot from a couple angles. Lyndsey's huge eyes gave her a sad, waif-like appearance. *Just perfect.* "That should do it."

Jeri lowered her voice and leaned close. "Don't pass this around, but I found out something about the fire that I'm adding to my article." She glanced over her shoulder. "The fire marshal said the fire was *no accident.*"

Lyndsey's smile faded. "You mean ... someone started the fire on purpose?"

"Looks like it."

"Who would do something like that?"

"I don't know." Jeri rubbed her tiny pearl earring. "I wonder if somebody's mad at Ms. Todd. It was mostly the stuff on her desk that got burned. Maybe somebody she flunked is getting revenge?"

"Maybe." Lyndsey plucked at the blanket. "Others might not like her for different reasons." She paused. "Like the morning guard maybe. I heard them in the hallway once. He asked her out, and she turned him down. Maybe he's mad."

"Really?" They'd been together outside a few minutes ago. Was he asking again? "Well, don't tell anyone about it being arson," Jeri repeated. "I think I got the information first. I bet the *Lightning Bolt* publishes my article now." If so, it would be Jeri's second article in there.

On the way to her next class, Jeri stopped in the basement of Herald House at the newspaper office. It didn't even smell like smoke down there. No one would guess that just an hour ago there'd been a smoky fire three floors overhead.

Jeri waited at the long wooden counter that ran the length of the room instead of pushing through the swinging door to the newsroom. Claire, the junior editor, continued to work, bent over her large, scarred desk. Jeri bet she'd seen her come in and was ignoring her. Claire had made it clear that sixth graders were neither talented nor welcome on the staff. So when the *Lightning Bolt* advisor had hired Jeri a month ago anyway, Claire was forced to tolerate Jeri's presence. And she resented it.

Jeri cleared her throat. "Claire?" When she got no response, she repeated her name louder.

"What?" Claire snapped, peering over her tiny glasses. "Where'd you come from?"

"From the fire. It was my biology lab that caught fire this morning." She took the plunge. "I could write a good eyewitness piece about it for the paper."

Claire stuck her pen behind her ear, shoved her chair back, and sauntered up to the counter. Today her long red hair was in a braid down her back. Very efficient, Jeri thought. "It's already covered. Stick to your beat, Lois Lane."

"I don't have anything to report on for Spanish or French Club," Jeri protested, "but I've got a *great* story about the fire and a photo of a girl in my class who put it out."

Claire shook her head and rolled her eyes. "The *fire's* the story, not some little sixth-grade girl." She turned her back on Jeri. "You've got a lot to learn, kid."

I guess so, Jeri thought as she left for her next class. *But so do you, Claire.* Just because the *Lightning Bolt* junior editor didn't want her article didn't mean it wouldn't get published. And soon.

3
WHERE THERE'S SMOKE . . .

By lunchtime, Jeri noticed that her throat hardly
hurt anymore. Being out in the hall at the time of the
explosion had kept her from serious harm. She only
wished Abby and Lyndsey had been as far from the
smoke and flames.

At the dining hall Jeri spotted her house mother
standing under the massive chandelier in the entryway.
"Ms. Carter, do you know how Abby's doing?"

"Yes." She wrapped her arm around Jeri's shoulders,
walking with her over to the French doors that opened
onto a balcony. "You'll be glad to hear that the
bronchoscope showed little damage. The medicine seems
to be controlling the cough." Sheer white curtains waved
in the slight breeze from the window. "They want to keep
her overnight for observation though."

"Can we go visit her?"

She shook her head, but her short, sculpted hair stayed perfectly in place. "No student visitors, the doctor said. Anyway, it hurts her to talk." At Jeri's sigh, she added, "I'm taking a bouquet of carnations over tonight. If you'd like to send her a get-well card, I'll take it with me."

"I'll make one right after school," Jeri said.

Although Rosa and Nikki were already near the front of the lunch line, Jeri went to the end. While they ate, Jeri would talk to them about making cards for Abby. Nikki and Abby were roommates, although the petite blonde from England and the tall sturdy American horsewoman couldn't have been more different. After they made the get-well cards, Jeri would put together a special edition of their newspaper with the news about the fire on the front page.

Let's see, I'll use my arson article and Nikki's write-up about her dressage competition. Rosa, always the social butterfly, could write some more advice about next weekend's Hawaiian luau and dance ...

Gradually, from a group ahead of her in the lunch line, Jeri became aware of Tim's name being tossed around. The voices of Lisa Poole and her friends carried clearly as they made fun of him.

"Let me see!" Melinda Rabb, her cheeks and hands bright pink, grabbed a piece of paper with a drawing on it.

Jeri craned her neck and saw a portrait of a girl with long blondish hair and even longer earrings. Huge beads around her neck spelled LISA.

"Cool, Poole! It looks just like you!" Melinda snickered and held it up for others to see.

"Give that back," Lisa hissed, her face mottled an unbecoming red.

Someone asked, "Are you going to frame it?"

"Maybe Tim will autograph it for you. He'll put, 'All my love, Tim'!"

"Shut up, you guys!"

Lisa was mean enough by herself, Jeri thought, but the teasing from her so-called friends made her even worse.

Lisa tore the portrait in half, then in half again, and then threw the pieces at them. "Wait till that dork decides he likes one of *you*!"

"No chance. He's madly in love with you," Melinda said. She made a kissing noise on the back of her chapped hand.

Jeri fumed. Why did they have to talk that way about Tim? He couldn't help being mentally impaired, and he was always really nice to people, which was more than she could say for those snobby girls. *If Tim treated me special, I'd be a lot nicer to him than Lisa.* Tim had a heart and feelings like anyone else. All the special needs kids did.

The other three students from New Hope Academy—Carl, Cindy, and Linda—worked there in the dining hall. Cindy served the rolls, and Carl and Linda scraped dirty plates in the kitchen. According to Tim, Carl and Linda liked working back there, but Cindy disliked her job. It was easy for Jeri to see why. Up ahead, Lisa and Melinda made faces at the girl with Down syndrome. Jeri wished The Head would catch those two and nail them.

"Thanks, Cindy," Jeri said when she was given her cloverleaf wheat roll. "Have a good day." She was pleased to see Cindy break into a big smile.

Nikki and Rosa were half done with their chicken fried steak and mashed potatoes when Jeri set her tray next to theirs. "Did you know Abby was in the hospital?" she said right away.

"Ms. Carter just told us." Rosa buried three pats of butter in her potatoes despite her constant lament that she was gaining weight. "I thought she was in the infirmary."

"I was there when the ambulance came," Jeri said. "Let's make her some get-well cards after school. Ms. Carter said she'd deliver them."

Nikki took Rosa's leftover steak and began cutting it up. "She'll want her backpack too. I'll fill it with books she's been reading." Nikki reached for the steak sauce. "I could loan her my DVD player and some movies too."

"Perfect." Jeri wished she could make offers like that, but she didn't have that kind of money. Nikki, though, had her own horse boarding at the school, her own computer and fancy printer/fax, an MP3 player, and a personal DVD player.

Jeri sprinkled her entire meal liberally with salt. "I'm putting together a special edition of our paper tonight too," she said.

Nikki dabbed at the steak sauce on her sleeve. "I wrote up the dressage competition if you want that," she said, referring to her special riding classes. "The photos you took of me on Show Stopper last Saturday turned out great."

"It's cool watching you perform." *Dressage* was so graceful that Jeri knew why it was sometimes called "horse ballet." Although just a sixth grader, Nikki always took prizes in Landmark's competitions with other schools. Nikki was stocky and sometimes clumsy in her cowboy boots, but on the back of her horse she was what Ms. Carter called "poetry in motion." Jeri pointed her knife at Nikki. "I bet you make it to the Olympics before you're fifteen."

"My *croupade* and *levade* still need work." Nikki dipped her napkin in her water glass and scrubbed her sleeve. "My *capriole* and *courbette* are better though."

"Do we have to speak horsey language at lunch?" Rosa asked, her white smile dazzling against her dark skin.

"*Horsey* language?" Nikki's eyebrow arched high. "Those are very difficult dressage moves where the horse leaps above the ground. Like in that Lipizzan stallion movie I showed you."

"Well, ex*cuse* me." Rosa waved at a couple of upperclassmen who strolled by.

"Listen up. Back to the special edition," Jeri said. "I got a photo of Lyndsey Powers in the infirmary to go with the fire story." She lowered her voice and leaned over the table, telling them what she'd overheard the fire marshal say.

"A lighter?" Rosa stirred her milk with her straw. "That's how it started?"

"Yup. I guess if you leave them burning long enough, they can overheat and explode. Keep it a secret till tomorrow though. I want to beat the *Lightning Bolt* to the story. Claire didn't want my article, but when she reads it, she's gonna be sorry she turned it down."

After changing out of their uniforms after school, they met in Jeri and Rosa's room to make a giant cardboard get-well card for Abby. Nikki printed out some photos of English castles and cottages she found on the Internet and pasted them on the card. "That should look like home to her," she said, adding a picture of Buckingham Palace.

Ms. Carter popped in then, her lavender nylon running suit making swishing noises. Evenings and weekends, Ms. Carter was ready to jog at a moment's notice. Jeri figured that's why she was such a calm house mother—she was always taking off for ten minutes to run off some steam.

After Ms. Carter left, Jeri tucked her bare foot underneath her and opened her Publisher software. In the ninety minutes until supper, she planned to put the paper together. Her photo of Lyndsey smiling bravely while holding her bandaged arm, was the perfect touch for the front page.

"Here's my column," Rosa said, handing Jeri several scribbled scraps of notes. Although Rosa was barely over five feet tall, her pink tee proclaimed *I'm big in Japan!*

Jeri sighed. If only Rosa would type things up. Oh well … the *Dear Rosa* column continued to be the part every girl read first. Jeri squinted to decipher the flowery, loopy writing. "I can't read this!" Jeri said, tossing the requests for advice on her desk.

"Are you blind or what?"

"Who taught you to write?" Jeri shot back. "Could you just read them to me—*slowly*—and I'll type them in?"

"I guess." Rosa snatched them up and sank gracefully onto her bed, which was covered with a giraffe-print bedspread and stuffed tigers and leopards. "This week's questions are all about the luau."

Rosa was the sixth-grade representative on the planning committee for the Hawaiian luau and dance. Both the Landmark School for Girls and the Patterson School for Boys were invited. Only nine days away, it would be held in Gracey Park in Landmark Hills.

"Okay, ready? First note." She read syllable by slow syllable. "'Dear Rosa: What if no boy invites me to the luau? I don't want to be a wallflower.'" Rosa bounced lightly on the bed, swinging her legs clad in flared jeans. "Here's my answer: 'Not a problem, Wallflower. Dates aren't needed. Be free! Hang with your GFs. Then you can dance with all the guys!'"

Well, Jeri thought, *that advice works for Rosa anyway.* Guys swarmed around her wherever she went—church, the mall, the movies. Jeri and Abby never had that problem. "Okay, next note." Jeri's fingers were poised above the keyboard.

"Second note says, 'Dear Rosa: I feel stupid when everyone's talking about the luau. What's a luau anyway?' Here's the answer: 'Dear Clueless: Think beaches and pineapples. Think the bend-over-backwards limbo and flowery dresses and bamboo torches. Think lei necklaces and surfboards.'"

"Good description," Jeri said, typing quickly.

"This last one's—"

"Wait a minute." Jeri typed the last three lines, then nodded.

"This last girl's having a panic attack. It says, 'How can I learn hula dancing by next week? Impossible!!!!!' That's with five exclamation marks. I told her this: 'Dear Hyper: Don't despair! Check out the library DVDs on hula dancing. Also, before the dance starts at the luau, someone's giving lessons. You won't be learning the dances alone. Get gutsy—and get out there!'"

"Good advice, as always," Jeri said, typing the last bit. "I think the whole school's going to the hoedown."

Rosa tossed her scribbled pages onto her desk. "I wish Ms. Carter allowed us to have dates for the dance. I turned down *two* high-school guys at church last week!"

Jeri turned around slowly and faced her. "Oh, I feel so sorry for you. Personally, I'm *glad* we don't need dates for the dance." Jeri figured no one would ask her, for one thing. Anyway, she was too young, with or without Ms. Carter's rules.

"Come on, Jer. There must be *someone* you want to dance with," Rosa said. "They're having regular dances—not just hula."

Jeri turned back to her computer so Rosa couldn't read the truth on her face. There *was* someone special … but it was a secret. No one knew she cared, including the boy … and Rosa—*especially* Rosa. After the way Rosa had "helped" Abby last winter, Jeri had sworn herself to secrecy.

It was before Christmas when Abby confided that she liked a boy at church. Rosa had decided to play matchmaker. Jeri knew she meant to help, but she badgered Abby about cutting her hair in a new style and wearing makeup and learning to flirt. Abby had refused. ("That's so not me," she'd protested.) After that, Rosa took charge herself. She told the boy Abby liked him and gave him Abby's phone number. He never called, but when Abby found out what Rosa had done, she nearly died of shame.

That's not going to happen to me! Jeri vowed.

She stared at her computer screen without seeing any of the words. Her crush's name was Dallas Chandler. He attended Patterson, and he came from Ft. Worth, Texas. In Sunday school class when he talked about their cattle ranch back home, she loved listening to his soft southern drawl.

The thing Jeri admired most was that he wasn't embarrassed to admit he read his Bible nearly every day. And when he was asked to pray in class, he didn't stumble over his words like the other boys.

"Here's my piece," Nikki said, nudging the bedroom

door open with her cowboy boot. "I emailed you the picture files."

Jeri blinked, jerked out of her pleasant Dallas daydream. Nikki's article, printed in all capital letters on a torn-out sheet of notebook paper, wasn't much easier to read than Rosa's handwriting. Jeri sighed. Being the editor wasn't as glamorous as she'd expected when they started the paper.

"Thanks. I'll download the photos in a minute."

An hour later, the paper was done and proofed. Luckily Jeri already had Abby's article on "Music to Change Your Mood." Except for weeding out the British expressions no one here understood, Abby's articles were turned in nearly perfect.

On Friday morning, after making copies at the media center, Jeri bought a copy of the *Lightning Bolt* to see how the senior reporter covered the fire. While standing in the breakfast line, she eagerly scanned the front page. The fire wasn't even mentioned. Impossible! An inside page, however, held a small column that only referred to an accident in the biology lab. Most of the article told how to prevent fires.

Boy, some reporter really fell down on the job, Jeri thought. That fire was no accident. Once Mrs. Gludell, the advisor for the school paper, saw Jeri's account of the fire—complete with photos—she'd see what a waste it was having Jeri cover Spanish Club.

Rosa still hadn't arrived for breakfast by the time Jeri finished her blueberry bagel and scrambled eggs. Jeri gave away her own published newspaper to twenty sixth graders and half a dozen seventh graders. Just as she'd predicted, they were immediately drawn to the photo of Lyndsey, all bandaged in her hospital bed. This time *her* story on the unknown arsonist got more attention than the "Dear Rosa" column.

Jeri stopped at the McClellan House table. "Where's Lyndsey?" she asked.

"Staying in bed today," one girl said. "Want me to give her your paper?"

Jeri thought a moment. "No, I'll stop by her room later."

On the way to her biology lecture—thankfully *not* held in the lab—she reread her own account of the fire. She smiled to herself. Unless she missed her guess, soon The Head and Mrs. Gludell would be *begging* her to be the *Lightning Bolt's* first investigative reporter.

Glad that the rain had passed, Jeri skirted shallow puddles on the way to her biology lecture. She wondered what Ms. Todd would have to say about yesterday. *I'll give her a copy of my paper. Then she'll see what a hero Lyndsey was. She might even apologize for snarling at her yesterday.*

As Jeri rounded the corner of Poplar Hall, she caught a whiff of smoke. Pivoting in alarm, she looked up at the building, then around the bushes and in the doorway. Where was the smell coming from? Heart pounding, she braced herself for another explosion.

Then she spotted the security guard leaning against the back side of the marble George Washington statue. He was puffing on a cigarette. Jeri eyed him closely. Short and round, he stretched his brown uniform shirt so tight it gapped in the front. His bristly mustache resembled a dirty toothbrush, and he'd missed a patch of whiskers when shaving that morning. If he'd really wanted to date Ms. Todd, it was no surprise to Jeri that she'd turned him down. Still, it was hard to believe he could be mad enough to burn her classroom.

Jeri cleared her throat. "Hi."

The guard swung around and dropped his cigarette, grinding it under his heel. "Don't want any more fires, do we?" he asked.

"No. I was wondering ... Early yesterday morning, did you see anyone hanging around Herald Hall before first period?"

"The fire marshal asked me that yesterday."

Jeri waited. "Can you tell me too, or is it some kind of secret?"

He squinted at her as if puzzled—or suspicious. "Why don't you leave investigating to the officials?"

"It's personal. Two of my friends were hurt. One's even in the hospital."

"Oh. Sorry." He patted his shirt pocket where he kept a pack of cigarettes, then thought better of it. "About who I saw yesterday ... it was just the usual. Tim was mopping,

Mr. Rankin was showing him what to do, kids were going in, two of the teachers were talking …"

"Did you let Mr. Rankin into the building?"

"Well, I unlocked it earlier on my rounds." He jingled a ring of keys hanging from his belt loop. "Normal procedure at six thirty."

"Oh. So you were at work before the fire started?"

He shifted his weight. "I was here all night. I work the night shift. New employees get the worst hours."

"Are you new?"

"Been here four months." He yawned so wide Jeri could see his molars. "Sorry. I work midnight to ten. I'm heading home soon."

Jeri shifted her backpack to her other shoulder. If only she had the guts to ask him about trying to date her teacher. "Um, there's something else … I mean … I heard …"

"What?"

She blushed. "Nothing."

"Go ahead. Spit it out."

She stared at her feet, unable to look at his face. How should she phrase it? *Did you feel so rejected that you torched Ms. Todd's lab?*

"I'd better get to class," she finally said.

Burning with embarrassment, Jeri made it to the lecture hall fifteen seconds before the tardy-bell rang. She hadn't really learned anything new from the security guard.

Jeri frowned. That security guard was in a perfect

position to start fires himself. He had keys to every building. He worked early morning hours when most people were still asleep. If Lyndsey was right, he had a personal grudge against their biology teacher. And he smoked. Jeri bet he was carrying a lighter in his pocket right this very minute.

If there was ever another fire, she'd be checking on that security guard's whereabouts first thing.

4
FIRE BUG

As the day wore on, the full impact of the fire hit Jeri. Someone at the school—probably someone she knew—had deliberately set fire to the biology lab. Abby could have been in a severe burn unit in the hospital—or worse. Jeri and her friends couldn't wait till she was released.

After school, they made a "Welcome Back, Abby!" banner to tape to her bedroom door. Rosa got permission from the house mother to have a tiny party in the lounge when Ms. Carter brought her home. Hopefully the chocolate-covered ice cream bars and fruity popsicles would appeal to someone with a sore throat. After their little party, Jeri planned to take a copy of her newspaper to Lyndsey's dorm.

They were waiting for Abby downstairs when the

doorbell rang. Nikki answered the door. After a moment, she appeared in the doorway and caught Jeri's eye. "Somebody to see you," she said, her lips twitching.

Tim stepped around her and, beaming, advanced into the room. He banged into an end table and rattled the stained-glass lamp, then headed straight toward Jeri. Grinning, he held out a gift bag covered with yellow baby chicks and ducks. Yellow tissue paper stuck out the top.

"Hi, Jeri! Happy Easter early!" Tim said, handing her the bag.

Jeri stared, frozen to the spot. Several girls drifted in from the kitchen and study room to see who'd come. Someone behind Jeri hummed *dum, dum, de-dum; dum, dum, de-dum* of the "Wedding March." She forced her stiff lips to smile. "Hi, Tim. How'd you get here?"

"Mom drove me out after school."

"Oh." Her face radiated heat, and when someone snickered, grew hotter still. "Is that bag for me?"

"Yes. Lisa didn't want it. She's not nice like you."

"Thank you," Jeri said. *God, what do I do?* She didn't want to push him away like Lisa, but this was humiliating, especially in front of everyone! She caught Rosa's sympathetic glance and raised eyebrows. They all probably felt sorry for her. Well, they'd admire her if she kept her cool. She took the gift bag. "I'll save it. Can you believe Easter's just two weeks away?"

"No, open it now," he said, whipping the yellow tissue

paper out himself. "Look!" He reached in the bag and lifted out a white stuffed bunny with gray floppy ears wearing a white eyelet baby bonnet. "This is Powder Puff. You can bend her legs and ears. She sits up." Several girls behind Jeri broke into giggles.

"That's really cute, Tim." Jeri bent its ears back and forth and wished the floor would open up and swallow her. "Happy Easter to you too." *And now go away!*

Tim peered over her shoulder. "Where's Abby?"

"She had to go to the hospital yesterday," Rosa said, "but she's getting back soon. We're having a little welcome-home party for her."

Tim's face fell. "I didn't bring Abby a present. I like her."

Jeri brightened. "You can give Abby the bunny."

"No, that's yours." Tim grinned at the group gathered in the doorway. "Jeri's my girlfriend."

I am not! Jeri screamed inwardly. Miss Barbara lumbered into the room then, took Tim's arm, and guided him down the hall. "I imagine someone's waiting for you, right?" she asked.

"My mom is. She got the gift bag, but I picked out the bunny."

As soon as the front door shut behind him, the room exploded with whistles and shrieks. Mariah whispered in Jeri's ear, "How perfect. Now you have *two* honey bunnies!"

Jeri gritted her teeth, wishing she could smack Mariah.

"Jeri's got a boyfriend!"

"Is he your date to the luau?"

"Lisa's gonna be jealous that you stole her crush!"

"Ignore them," Rosa whispered as the girls drifted back to whatever they'd been doing. "You were nice to Tim. That's what counts."

Easy for you to say, Jeri thought. It's not exactly the same as having *cute* boys begging for your attention.

"She's right," Nikki said. "You did the right thing."

Did the right thing ...

It was good that no one could read her mind. *If only I'd been gone when Tim came.* She'd never hear the end of this. She'd like to talk to Mom, but Mom would agree with Rosa and Nikki. She'd always taught Jeri to do what the Bible said, no matter how hard it was. And Jeri knew the Bible said believers weren't supposed to look down on others or show favoritism. What was *inside* was the part that counted most.

It wasn't easy though, Jeri thought. She agreed with Mom, but somehow she'd thought people would admire her for being kind to Tim—not laugh at her. They had to know it was hard. Jeri looked at Powder Puff, the bunny. She almost regretted being Tim's friend now. *God, I'm sorry.*

Her thoughts were cut off by a weak but cheery, "I'm back!" Jeri gladly tucked the bunny into the bag and set it behind the love seat. She, for one, was thrilled to make Abby the center of attention now.

After Abby got settled on the couch, Jeri and Nikki brought her an ice-cream bar and a frozen-fruit bar, but Jeri noticed that she ate very little. "Are you really okay?" Jeri asked her.

"Just tired." Abby laid a hand at her neck. "My throat's still awfully sore."

Rosa sat on the arm of the couch. "You must have breathed in a ton of smoke."

"That's part of it," she said. "But that instrument the doctor put down my throat scraped it." She swallowed then, with obvious pain. "I'm just glad they finally sent me home."

"Did they call your mom?" Jeri asked.

"Yes, and Mum called me at the hospital last night and today. It hurt to talk though." She stood slowly. "I think I'll crawl into bed."

"Good idea." Jeri watched her slowly climb the stairs with Nikki, worried by the change in her. If the doctor sent Abby home, she must be well enough. But was the exhaustion normal? If only there was some way to help her feel better …

Jeri had wanted to quiz Abby about the fire that night, but obviously it would have to wait till tomorrow. Abby was an eyewitness, and she might have seen something suspicious without even knowing it. Abby would soon know the fire was arson. Jeri'd put a copy of their paper on her bed earlier.

Waves of sudden exhaustion washed over Jeri. Glancing out the window, she was surprised to see dusk had settled in already. Jeri sighed. Maybe she'd just wait till morning to take Lyndsey a copy of her newspaper. She'd rather sit back and watch a DVD with Rosa instead.

On Saturday morning, Abby was still asleep when Jeri finished her cold cereal in the dorm kitchen. Nikki had left early for the horse barn to work on her dressage competition, and few of the other girls—including Rosa—were even out of bed. Jeri grabbed her windbreaker and newspaper and headed to McClellan Hall.

Lyndsey's sixth-grade dorm was built on the edge of campus. Mostly glass and concrete, it contrasted sharply with Jeri's brick dorm with ivy-covered walls. Hampton House might be old, with its clunky radiators, open-beamed ceilings, and stone fireplace, but Jeri preferred it. That was good—no way could Mom afford the room and board in the new dorm anyway.

When she stepped inside McClellan, the house mother said Lyndsey was gone, but would be back shortly. "She's rescheduling a horseback riding lesson. Feel free to wait here."

"Thanks." Jeri gazed around the spacious game room. It had two Ping-Pong tables, a blinking juke box, three snack machines, and a large screen TV!

"You looking for Lyndsey?" a nasal voice said behind her.

Jeri turned to find a girl in gray sweats that she recognized from gym class. "Flannery, right?"

"Right." She blew her red nose. "Want me to take you to Lyndsey's room? It's next to mine."

"Okay. I have something for her."

"This way." Flannery led her to an elevator. "We're on the fourth floor."

Flannery balanced her bag of corn chips and two Hershey bars while she punched the fourth-floor button. Jeri barely felt the elevator glide upward before it coasted to a smooth stop and opened its doors. A high-school girl in a fuchsia jogging suit whacked Jeri with her tennis racquet when she got on.

Jeri rubbed her arm, stepped out of the elevator, and started down the long bare hallway. Flannery knocked on a door covered with a life-sized poster of a young movie star. "Hey, Alexis, you got company."

Blaring music was suddenly muffled. Shuffling footsteps approached, and a tall, beanpole-thin girl in striped pj's opened the door. Staring at Jeri from top to bottom, she sniffed. "You're looking for *me*?"

"Well, Lyndsey actually."

"I should've guessed." She turned her back on Jeri and crawled into a macraméd chair that hung from the ceiling like a hammock. She curled her feet underneath her.

"Jeri's gonna wait here for Lyndsey," Flannery said, giving Jeri a push into the room. She backed out and closed the door.

Alexis looked at her through half-closed eyes. "Whatever."

Jeri wished she'd waited downstairs. Pretending an interest in their view, she walked to the window and gazed out over the tops of trees. "I can see into the top of the clock tower from up here," she said.

"I'm sure that's thrilling for you," Alexis drawled.

Jeri stared at the floor, embarrassed at sounding like a baby, then turned and surveyed the room. Their bedspreads, chairs, rugs, and pillows were neon orange and lime green—pretty, but it probably glowed in the dark. She pulled a copy of her newspaper from her pocket. "Which is Lyndsey's desk?" she asked.

Alexis rolled her eyes. "Take a wild guess."

Jeri laid the paper on the desk covered with photos of Lyndsey's family—on the beach, in front of a Christmas tree, and Rollerblading. Lyndsey looked young in the pictures. Jeri leaned close. "Cute little sister. Does her family visit?"

"I've never seen them," Alexis said. "She flies home instead." Then, without another word, she put on headphones, closed her eyes, and sang along with her music.

Jeri returned to the window. She envied all the space they had: room enough for beds and desks, plus a love seat in the corner, a white metal bird cage with two parakeets, and a card table holding some art project.

Beside the window, a silky paisley scarf covered something on an easel. Jeri glanced at Alexis, who was still in a musical trance, and then lifted the cloth. Underneath was a painting—a portrait. A small photo was pinned to the upper corner of the easel. It was unmistakably a picture of Lyndsey's little sister.

Without warning, the door opened and closed, making the silky cloth flutter. Jeri whirled around, feeling guilty at being caught peeking. "Hi, Lyndsey," she said, gesturing at the painting. "This is really good."

Lyndsey moved across the room and covered it. "Thanks, but I don't let people see my work. I'm giving it to Mom for her birthday next month."

"You're really talented." Jeri pointed at Alexis, who was still tuning them out. "She said I could wait for you."

"I went to cancel my riding lesson. The cut on my arm hurts too much to handle the reins."

"I brought you something." Jeri grabbed the paper from Lyndsey's desk. "There you are. Front-page hero."

"Actually, Flannery showed me a copy last night." She read the article aloud slowly. "This is good," she said, looking up. "You wrote that? Thanks!"

"You want an extra copy for your parents?"

A shadow passed over Lyndsey's face. "No, I don't think so."

"Why? They'd be real proud of you."

"They'd be even more scared." She shook her head. "Mom would agree with Ms. Todd that what I did was too dangerous. I just didn't think about it at the time." Lyndsey plopped down in an orange director's chair and read more of the paper. "I like Rosa's column. Do you know what you're wearing to this luau thing?"

"Orange cut-off shorts and an orange flowered shirt from the second-hand store." She grinned. "Rosa calls me a bargain babe and says that I should write an article called 'Diva on a Dollar.' You're gonna go, aren't you?"

"Yeah, but I can't hula or anything." Lyndsey tapped the paper. "I didn't know our library had dancing videos."

"I checked out a couple. Want to come over and practice now?" Jeri asked. "Abby came home from the hospital last night too. I bet she'd like a visitor."

"I have laundry in a dryer downstairs to fold first. Can I come when I'm done?"

"Sure. See you later." Outside, the sun had gone under the clouds, and a stiff wind had turned the day gusty. *Great day for kites,* Jeri thought. For a Saturday, few girls were outside. Head down into the wind, Jeri jogged all the way to Hampton House.

She started upstairs as Rosa came running down. "Jeri! Where've you been? I hunted all over for you!"

"Why? What happened?"

"It's Abby. She had some kind of relapse. When she woke up this morning, she was too weak to get out of bed or eat anything." She leaned against the banister. "They called an ambulance and took her back to the hospital." Rosa's face clouded over, and her voice was barely a whisper. "I was so scared. Abby was awfully pale and weak."

"Was she coughing bad again?"

"No. Ms. Carter called it a toxic reaction to smoke. They did a blood test. 'Toxic gases in the blood,' I think she said. It can take as long as two days before the poison starts working in your body. That's what Ms. Carter said."

"Poison!"

"I don't really get it—something about oxygen shortages starving your cells. The ambulance guy said stuff found in smoke can be poisonous in your body. It was making her sicker."

"Makes sense. She was closest to the explosion," Jeri said, "and in the burning lab the longest."

"Plus she was sick with the flu all last week and probably run down," Rosa added.

"I wish I'd been here," Jeri said softly. "Can we go see her?"

"Not tonight. Miss Barbara's staying all night with her though."

They were still hanging out in the lounge twenty minutes later when Lyndsey showed up. "What a homey place," she said, taking in the crackling fire in the fireplace, the open oak stairway, and padded rocking chairs.

Jeri sank down into one of the rockers. "Sorry, but I'm not in the mood to practice hula dancing now. Abby just got taken back to the hospital. The smoke did something to her blood."

"Oh. I understand." Lyndsey stood awkwardly, shifting from one foot to the other. "I should probably just go." She turned and headed down the hall.

"Wait," Jeri said, feeling guilty for cancelling after inviting her over. "I'll walk you part way. I need to pick up a library book that's on hold."

They were quiet as they started back. Jeri couldn't get Rosa's words out of her mind. Abby was *poisoned* by something in the smoke. What if there wasn't a cure? What if cells starved of oxygen had permanent damage? And what cells? *Brain* cells? Could Abby end up like the kids from New Hope Academy?

"I hope Abby comes home later today," Lyndsey said. "I didn't know smoke could hurt you even after a fire's out." Her voice caught as if she might choke. "If only I'd gotten her out of the lab sooner. I never saw her behind Ms. Todd's desk."

"That's not your fault," Jeri said. "You did more than anyone would—"

"Look!" Lyndsey yelled, pointing to a large wooden storage shed set back from the road.

Jeri turned where she pointed, started, then looked again. Through a side window, an orange reflection flickered and danced. It almost looked like—

"Fire!" Jeri screamed.

5
THE SCENE OF THE CRIME

Jeri took off running to the shed that was set well back from the access road. She scanned the area for a teacher or security guard, but no one was out on this blustery Saturday except a couple girls on bikes and one carrying an armful of books. Two other students stopped in the drive to gawk.

Following right on Jeri's heels, Lyndsey ran to the storage building. She peered in a small window next to the door, her hands cupped around her eyes and forehead pressed to the glass. "Looks like a lawn mower's on fire." She reached for the doorknob.

"Don't go in there! Not again!" Jeri said. "Call 9–1–1." At Lyndsey's hesitation, she gave her a push. "Go back to my dorm and call!"

Lyndsey turned and raced in the direction of

Hampton House. Jeri peered in the same window, but she couldn't distinguish what was on fire. There was too much smoke to make it out.

She couldn't see anyone, but Tim had told her that he cleaned the lawn mowers and snow blowers stored there. Was Tim in there now? Was he overcome by smoke and lying behind the mower? Was he dying from smoke inhalation while she waited safely outside for the fire department to arrive?

"Tim! Are you in there?" she yelled.

When there was no answer, she glanced over her shoulder. Where was Lyndsey? Or her house mother? If Tim—or Mr. Rankin—was lying in that burning building, was there really time to wait for anyone? To fuel the mowers and snow blowers, there must be cans of gasoline in there. If the fire reached them, the explosion would blow up the building—and anyone trapped inside.

She had to do something. Spying a water spigot on the side of the building, Jeri raced to it and tried to twist the knob. It didn't budge. She kept trying, but nothing trickled out at all. Was it rusted shut?

Running back to the window, she peered inside again. Rows of tools and loops of rope and garden hose hung on the back wall. In the middle of the tools was a fire extinguisher.

She didn't have any choice. Jeri yanked the door open and smoke rushed out. Inside, peering through tiny slits, she groped for the light switch and flipped it on. One light flicked on, but the weak light barely penetrated the smoke.

Running to the back wall, she unhooked the red fire extinguisher. The metal cylinder was so heavy she nearly dropped it. According to the diagram on its side, it had to be turned upside down to work. Then you pointed the attached hose at the fire.

Jeri's eyes stung as she up-ended the extinguisher, moved near the blaze, and squeezed the nozzle. A stream of foamy bubbles overshot the fire altogether. She moved a bit closer, held the nozzle tighter, and aimed again. This time a full load of frothy bubbles landed on the flames. She squinted, aimed, and squeezed, closing her eyes against the smoke and blistering heat.

After holding her breath long enough to empty the contents on the blaze, Jeri couldn't see any more flames. Dropping the extinguisher with a clatter, she fanned the smoke away from her face and ran behind the mower. Its cushioned seat was charred, and the tires were melted. The mower itself was covered in foam. Jeri knelt and scanned the surrounding area.

No Tim. She let out the breath she'd been holding. No one at all was there.

Turning, she noticed a back door not far away. It stood ajar a couple inches. She opened it wide, gulped the cool fresh air, and glanced in all directions. No one was outside the back door. Had the arsonist set the fire and escaped this way? In the distance she heard the wailing siren of an approaching fire engine.

Stepping back inside, Jeri noticed several gasoline cans along another wall. Were they empty? Or just waiting for a blaze to touch them and set off an explosion? *Thank you, God, for helping me!*

"Jeri! Jeri!" Lyndsey yelled. "Are you all right?"

"I'm here." Jeri headed outside, her eyes streaming from the smoke. "I'm safe."

Lyndsey was surrounded by half a dozen girls and Ms. Carter.

"Jeri, what did you *do*?" the house mother cried, grabbing her in a bear hug. "You could have been killed!"

Jeri's face was muffled against Ms. Carter's front. "I was afraid Tim was inside. Or Mr. Rankin." She pulled away and looked up at her. "If the fire had reached the gasoline cans, there would've been a terrible explosion."

"How'd you know what to do?" the house mother asked.

"I saw the fire extinguisher on the wall," Jeri said.

Just then Nikki and Rosa ran up. "You shouldn't have gone in there," Nikki said. "You want to end up in the hospital like Abby? Breathing smoke is dangerous!"

Rosa grabbed Jeri's arm. "What were you thinking of, girl? You wanna be fried?"

"I have to agree with Nikki and Rosa," Ms. Carter said. "I understand why you did it. But *please*, don't do this again!" She turned to Lyndsey. "*Either* of you."

Conversation was cut short as a yellow fire truck pulled up on the grass next to the shed. Two firefighters jumped out and shouted, "Stand back!" Then they headed inside. One opened the shed door, dispersing the smoke. Jeri shook her head. Why hadn't she thought of that?

By now a crowd had gathered, and Jeri spotted The Head striding across the grass. She arrived as the firefighters emerged from the shed, her upswept hairdo not even bending in the stiff breeze.

"What happened?" she demanded. "I'm the headmistress here."

"Ma'am, I'm afraid you've got a fire bug on your campus."

Her mouth tightened. "Be specific, young man."

"This fire was set deliberately too, with gasoline and rags. The point of origin was a lawn mower seat."

Not again! Jeri glanced at Lyndsey, who looked as sick as she felt.

"Couldn't it have been an accident?" The Head asked.

"Afraid not. The fire burns longest at the point of origin." He held up a charred piece of cloth. "This combustible material was found on the seat. It'd be very hard for a fire to start there accidentally. In an engine maybe—with an electrical problem. But not rags on the padded seat."

The Head frowned. "Have the fire marshal call me," she said and then left.

Ms. Carter studied Jeri carefully. "Maybe you should go to the infirmary, just in case."

"I'm fine. Really. Not even coughing." At the house mother's skeptical glance, she added, "I held my breath in there most of the time."

"If you don't feel well later, do you promise to tell me?"

Jeri nodded. "I promise."

"This creeps me out," Rosa said. "Two fires in two days. Both in broad daylight."

"And no one sees anything suspicious before the fires break out," Jeri added.

Lyndsey cast a guilty look in Jeri's direction and then turned around.

Jeri chewed her lower lip. "Rosa, I still gotta run to the library, and then I'll be right back."

"See you at the room," Rosa said, shivering and stamping her feet. "It's freezing out here."

Jeri pulled Lyndsey down the sidewalk. "What's going on? You're acting funny." She touched Lyndsey's arm. "Do you know something about the fire?"

"No," Lyndsey said. "Nothing." She was quiet for another minute, but as they drew near McClellan House, her footsteps slowed. "I don't really *know* anything about the fire."

Jeri frowned. "But you suspect something?"

Lyndsey scuffed her shoe back and forth on the sidewalk. "I'd hate to get an innocent person in trouble."

"What do you know?" When she remained silent, Jeri gripped her arm. "You have to tell! Did you see something?"

"It probably doesn't mean anything …" Lyndsey took a deep breath. "When I ran to your dorm to call 9–1–1, I looked over my shoulder to see if any flames were spreading to the roof. That's when I saw him."

"Saw who?"

She paused. "Tim."

"What was he doing?"

"Nothing really … except running away from the shed. He came from behind the building and headed toward the sports complex."

Jeri's heart sank as she remembered the back door open a few inches. "Are you sure it was Tim?"

"He was wearing that orange jacket with the owl on the back."

Jeri nodded. There was probably only one ugly jacket like that in the world. "Do you think he was coming out of the shed?"

"It seemed like it." Lyndsey looked troubled. "Maybe he started the fire by accident—playing with matches or something—and got scared and ran away."

Jeri knew that could easily have happened. And yet … the fireman was positive that the fire was set on purpose. What if Tim was the arsonist? Jeri's heart beat faster at the idea. Maybe he couldn't help it. Maybe his brain disorder also made him set fires.

Her heart nearly stopped. If that were true, he might be planning—or setting—his next fire already! There was already one girl in the hospital. "You have to tell the investi-gator, Lyndsey."

"But what if I'm wrong? Or what if he has a good reason for running away?" Lyndsey wrung her hands. "I don't want to get him in trouble. No real damage was done."

"Not this time, but people got hurt yesterday—including you! And what about next time? Whoever's starting the fires—whether it's Tim or someone else—will probably get sneakier. We were lucky yesterday and today. You can't ex-pect that to happen every time."

Lyndsey took a deep breath. "I'll tell The Head what I saw." She pulled her coat collar up higher. "First let's ask Tim what he was doing and why he ran away. Maybe there's a good explanation, and we won't have to say anything."

Jeri thought about it for a moment. She didn't want to falsely accuse Tim either. That would be mean. He got picked on too much as it was.

"This is what I'll do," Jeri finally said. "Wait in your dorm, and I'll look for him and ask him now." She chewed her lower lip. "If I can't find him soon, though, you'll have to talk to The Head. If we wait, who knows what will go up in flames next?"

6
WEB OF LIES

Jeri headed off across the Landmark campus toward the girls' sports complex. There, she spotted Mr. Rankin using a weed trimmer around the edges of the softball field. Man, what a cold windy day to work outside. She shivered, partly from cold and partly from fear. Did Mr. Rankin even know about the shed fire yet?

She entered the complex's dome-shaped building. To her right, through the glass, four girls played on the indoor tennis court; half a dozen on her left watched TV while on treadmills. Straight ahead, five were working on movements in a self-defense class. Where could Tim be?

Jeri was turning to leave when he emerged from the weights room. "Hi, Tim!" she called.

He jerked his head up, tensed as if to run, and then recognized Jeri. "Hi!" he called, his face lighting up.

"Whatcha doin'?"

"Cleaning mats. Mr. Rankin told me to."

"You work hard around here," Jeri said, trying to figure out how to bring up the fire. "I'd rather work outdoors than indoors though."

"Me too. I like to exercise the horses and scoop snow."

"And mow grass?" Jeri asked, watching his expression.

Tim's smile faded. "I can't. I just clean the mowers."

"Were you working on one today in the shed?" she asked quietly.

"No!" Tim backed away from her. "I was sweeping. I didn't touch them."

"Are you sure?" Jeri asked, feeling a bit sick. "Someone saw you running away from the shed earlier. Why would you run away from sweeping?"

Tim whipped his head from side to side, as if looking for escape.

Jeri took a deep breath. "It was right after a fire started."

"What fire?" boomed a deep voice.

Jeri jumped and whirled around. Mr. Rankin was stalking down the hall toward them.

"I didn't start no fire!" Tim cried.

"What fire?" Mr. Rankin demanded again. "What are you talking about?"

Jeri gulped and jammed her shaking hands into her jacket pockets. "There was a small fire at the shed where you keep the lawn mowers. I put it out with the fire extinguisher."

"Another fire? Was this one arson too?"

God, I don't want to say this! "Well … the fireman thought so," she admitted.

Mr. Rankin stared at Tim. "You were there this morning."

"I didn't start a fire!" Tim wailed. "I didn't!"

By this time, half a dozen whispering girls had appeared in the hall from the aerobics room and self-defense class.

Mr. Rankin folded his arms across his chest. "You said someone saw Mr. Norton here running away from the fire. Is that true?"

"Not exactly. She wasn't sure."

"She must have been pretty sure for you to question him."

Jeri took a deep breath. "She recognized his orange owl jacket."

Mr. Rankin glanced at Tim, who still wore the coat. "This calls for an investigation." He faced Tim. "If the fire marshal backs up what Jeri said, you're finished. You can't break machinery and then set fire to it to cover the evidence."

"I didn't!" Tim cried. "Don't take away my job!"

Without looking back, Mr. Rankin passed through the double glass doors and turned toward the administration building. Jeri's stomach twisted in a painful knot. Within five minutes, The Head would know about Tim leaving the scene of the fire. She'd also wonder why Jeri hadn't reported it right away herself. She turned back to Tim and was mortified to see tears in his eyes.

"I thought you were my girlfriend," he whispered.

"I'm your *friend*," Jeri corrected him. "I didn't mean for Mr. Rankin to react that way, but I *had* to ask you."

"What will I tell Mom?" Tim wailed. "She's proud of me working here!"

Jeri closed her eyes briefly. Oh, *why* hadn't she been more careful when she talked to him? Why had she blurted it out where anyone could overhear? This job meant everything to Tim—and she'd ruined it for him.

"I bet the fire marshal will figure it out fast," Jeri said, trying to sound confident. "You'll probably be back here working next week."

She touched his sleeve, but he jerked away. Brushing at the tears on his plump cheeks, he shuffled down the hall and out the door.

Feeling a bit light-headed, Jeri watched him go. She would be 100 percent responsible if he lost his job. What if he'd only run away because he was afraid of the fire, and he was too embarrassed to admit it? If only she could rewind the last fifteen minutes and do things differently.

If Mr. Rankin's attitude was any indication, Jeri was afraid people would be all too eager to believe Tim was guilty. After all, he was often picked on by the girls. The investigator could accuse him of taking revenge by burning buildings and trying to hurt them back.

Could that be true? *God, please don't let Tim be punished for something he didn't do.*

"Tim! Wait!" She ran after him, keeping his bright orange jacket in view. She was breathing hard by the time she caught up. "I want to talk to you."

He finally stopped. Pulling his ball cap low over his forehead, he crossed his arms over his chest.

"Listen to me," Jeri said quietly. "Mr. Rankin was mean to you. You're a good worker."

"No, I'm not."

"Sure you are! I see you working hard all the time."

"But I'm dumb."

"Why do you say that?"

Tim hesitated. A frightened look came into his eyes. "I tried to put oil in a lawn mower once, but I spilled it."

Jeri's heart quickened. "When did you do that?"

Tim stared at the ground, silent.

"When, Tim?"

He sighed. "This morning—but you can't tell!"

Jeri let out her breath slowly. "Come sit down." She motioned to a bench out of the wind under a nearby dogwood tree. The weak sun filtered down through the branches and newly formed leaves. Tim shuffled over and sat beside her. "Now tell me what happened."

Tim leaned his elbows on his knees and let his cap hang down between them. "I was sweeping the shed. Mr. Rankin had bought new oil. I decided to surprise him."

"By doing what?"

"Putting oil in the mowers." His shoulders slumped. "I spilled it all over." He looked up, pure fear on his round face. "I was scared. I ran away and hid in the horse barn."

Jeri waited. And waited some more. "Then what?"

He smiled lopsidedly. "I got hungry. My lunch box was in the shed. I went back to get it."

"Had you locked the shed up?" Jeri asked.

"Me?" Tim cocked his head to one side. "I don't have any keys."

Jeri nodded. So the shed was unlocked while Tim was hiding in the horse barn—unlocked and available to an arsonist.

"Did you get your lunch then?"

"No. I went in the back door. The mower was burning! The oil I spilled caught on fire somehow!"

"So you were scared and ran away?"

"Yes. I mean, no." He shuddered. "I wasn't scared of the fire. I was scared Mr. Rankin would blame me for it."

Jeri sighed. She could understand that. That must have been when Lyndsey saw him and recognized his jacket.

"I need to ask you something, Tim." Jeri slipped her arm through his so he wouldn't run. "The fireman said *someone* tossed a match on some rags on the mower. Was that someone you?"

"No! No!" He hit his head with his fists, over and over. "No, no, no!"

"Stop that!" Jeri grabbed both his hands and pulled them down. She held onto his wrists until he calmed down, and then let them go. "It's going to be all right, Tim. The investigators will find the truth."

Tim stared at the ground, silent. A few minutes later Jeri shivered, realizing suddenly how very cold she was. She ought to go pick up her library book, but she didn't need Tim following her there. Enough was enough for one day. She stood up. "I'm heading back to the dorm now."

"I'll come with you."

No! Jeri took a deep breath. "You don't need to do that. It's out of your way."

"I don't mind." He got up too. "I'm not mad at you anymore."

"That's good. I'm sorry you've had such a rotten day. Why don't you get your bike and head home?" Jeri walked backwards down the sidewalk toward her dorm, ignoring the curious stares of girls they passed.

"Tomorrow will be better," Tim said, running clumsily to catch up. "That's what Mom always says."

Jeri smiled. "Your mom sounds nice."

"She is." Tim leaned close and whispered, "Mom adopted me."

"*Really?*" Jeri said, embarrassed at the surprise in her voice. So his mom had known there was something wrong with Tim, and she wanted him anyway. She'd *chosen* him, problems and all.

"She says I'm special." Tim clapped suddenly. "You want to come home with me and see her?"

"I can't leave campus." At his crestfallen face, Jeri added, "I'm sorry."

"It's okay."

As they approached Hampton House, Jeri felt her stomach tighten into a knot. She hoped no one was looking out a window right now. She had already been teased about that stuffed bunny enough to last a lifetime. Luckily the rolling gray clouds threatened rain, or more girls would be outside Rollerblading and biking.

"Try to have a good Sunday tomorrow," Jeri said. "Maybe by Monday or Tuesday all this will be over." She turned to go in.

"Stop!" Tim grabbed Jeri's arm.

Jeri frowned. "I have to get going, Tim."

"I want to ask you something." Tim licked his lips, rubbed a hand back through his hair, and waved his ball cap back and forth. "Are you going to the whing-ding thing?"

Jeri laughed. "Whing-ding thing?" Then she saw he was serious. "You mean the luau next weekend?"

He nodded. "Carl and me—we're folding tables when it's over, so we get to come. Cindy and Linda get to come too."

"I'm helping decorate in the morning," Jeri said, surprised the New Hope kids would be there. "Then I'll go to the luau and dance later."

"Will you dance with me? And be my date?" Tim asked, grinning. He bounced up and down on the balls of his feet.

Your date? "Gee, Tim, that's nice of you to ask," she stammered.

"I can't drive. Mom will pick you up."

"Wait, Tim. I have to say no. I'm too young to date." It was true, and Jeri had never been more glad of the fact. "Mom won't let me, and neither will Ms. Carter. No sixth grader gets to have a date for the dance."

"Let's do everything else together then."

What had she gotten herself into? "I'm sure I'll see you there," she said slowly. "Either at the luau or watching the games. They're having funny events like coconut bowling and a tropical three-legged race and bobbing for seashells."

"Be my partner in the three-legged race then!" Tim said. "I'm fast!"

"I'm sure you are." Jeri sighed. She'd daydreamed for weeks that Dallas would be her partner in the race. He probably wouldn't ask, but he might. If she said yes to Tim, she'd be paired with him in front of both schools. She thought being kind to Tim would make her feel good—not eternally embarrassed.

Out of the corner of her eye, she studied Tim's hopeful expression. He'd already had such a rotten day. Being terrified when discovering the fire, then Mr. Rankin trying to get him fired from his job after she questioned Tim in front of him … Could she really add one more horrible thing to his day?

She could almost hear her mom's voice in her head. *Treat everyone with respect and make them feel valued*, she said. *You can't go wrong following the Golden Rule. "Do unto others, as you would have them do unto you."* Inwardly she sighed. *Help me, God. I want to do what's right.*

She forced herself to smile. "I'd be glad to be your racing partner. I bet we win!"

"I'll invite Mom to watch us. Then you can meet her."

Keep smiling. It'll be okay, she reassured herself. Tim deserved a break. He truly *was* one of the nicest, kindest boys she knew.

At least, she hoped so. If she was wrong about him, she'd just made a date with an arsonist.

7
TAKING THE HEAT

At loose ends, Jeri wandered around her dorm room Saturday afternoon, too agitated to settle down anywhere for long. After she jumped up for the fourth time during their movie, Rosa put it on pause. "Got ants in your pants or what?"

"Sorry." She plopped back down in the beanbag chair and focused on the laptop screen. However, her mind kept worrying about Abby in the hospital, Tim getting fired, the three-legged race, the arsonist striking next …

She jumped up again. "Let's get outside," she said. "Wanna go watch Nikki ride?"

"No way, José." Rosa shivered and pulled her comforter up to her neck. "The temperature dropped twenty degrees today."

Grabbing her heavy coat, Jeri dug in the pockets for gloves. "See you later." Outside, the wind blasted her, making her gasp. Rosa was right. It felt like spring had retreated back into winter in a matter of hours. Jeri considered going back for her stocking cap, but just covered her ears with her hands instead and struck out across campus. Walking fast helped her warm up, plus work off some nervous energy.

Soon her face was freezing though, and frigid air cut through her jeans. Up ahead was the Equestrian Center. It'd be cold in there too, but it'd be out of the wind. She might as well stop and watch Nikki practice. With the tri-state competition just ten days away, she practiced her dressage moves daily.

The riding ring was empty though, so Jeri headed to Show Stopper's stall. Nikki looked surprised to see her. "Hey! What's up?"

"Nothin'." Jeri leaned over the stall door. "Just bored, I guess." She had what her mom called *the fidgets*. She watched Nikki brush her horse for a minute. "I think I'll do that too. See ya." She headed around to the other side of the barn to where her rental horse, Prancer, had his stall. She rode him for her weekly lessons. She liked to pretend he belonged to her, but she actually shared him with a dozen other girls.

As she rounded the corner, the lanky stable hand emerged just ahead from the tack room.

"Hi there, Jer," Sam drawled, arms full with a saddle and blanket. "Y'all come to muck out stalls with me?"

"Sorry, no," she said, laughing. "Has Loretta had her kittens yet?"

"Nope. Any day now. She's big as a pig and has taken to hidin' in the oddest places."

"I'll keep an eye open for her."

Jeri filled a black bucket with water, got a plastic bowl of oats from the barrel, and then filled Prancer's hanging mesh bag with hay. After twenty minutes of brushing him, combing his mane and tail, and feeding him an apple from the bucket Sam always kept filled, she walked back to the dorm with Nikki.

Her turbulent feelings had settled some, at least enough to eat pizza and play four fast games of Ping-Pong with her friends. Even so, that night her fretful dreams were an odd mixture of Tim riding Prancer to the luau while she was fighting off the tentacles of a giant bean plant wrapped around her ankles.

On Sunday morning, Jeri and Rosa were rushing out the door to catch their ride to church when their phone rang. Jeri grabbed it. It was Abby.

"Hey there," Jeri said. "Are you coming home today? We didn't think they'd keep you overnight again."

"I hope they let me go soon. I feel better, just tired. Miss Barbara stayed with me last night." Abby giggled. "She's a hoot. When I couldn't sleep, she taught me a cool game called backgammon. You play it with chips and dice."

"You were *gambling* with Miss Barbara?" Jeri said, rolling her eyes at Rosa.

Abby laughed, which set off her coughing. "Not that kind of game," she finally said. "I bet you were just leaving for church. I guess I'll see you later."

They raced to catch their ride, but the minivan was already pulling out of the parking lot when Jeri flagged it down. She and Rosa squeezed into the last seats in the back.

Every Sunday morning, two minivans and a small bus took girls to the Landmark Hills Community Church. Jeri loved going to church, mostly because of the youth program there. The sixth graders' Sunday school teacher, Mr. Jenkins, made each student feel welcome ... even special. Jeri thought he understood girls almost as well as her mom. But then, he had five daughters of his own. A "thorn among the roses," he called himself.

Jeri pulled her coat close around her as they hurried from the van into the church. She'd already told Rosa what Mr. Rankin had said when he heard about the shed fire. "Since it's my fault if Tim loses his job, I want to put out a special edition. What do you think about asking people to come forward with information about the shed fire?"

Rosa hesitated. "Just be ready. You're gonna get teased big-time."

"I won't mention Tim's name or say it's to help him."

"I didn't want to tell you, but people know he's a suspect. Mr. Rankin—or somebody else—has been spreading the idea around. I heard people talking at breakfast."

Guilt washed over Jeri when she heard that. Mr. Rankin shouldn't be spreading rumors about Tim. Why was he so interested in pointing the finger at his helper anyway? Jeri tripped over her own feet as something occurred to her. *Mr. Rankin* had carried the mop water up to the third floor of Herald House—just before the fire broke out. *Mr. Rankin* had been in the shed showing Tim what to do earlier in the day. Had he started both fires then?

Was it possible? Was Mr. Rankin the arsonist—and determined to hang the crimes on Tim?

Rosa sailed through the open church door, her teal tier skirt swirling around her. "Hurry up," she called over her shoulder. Rosa might be right about the teasing if she published a request for information. Well, she'd just have to deal with the teasing when it happened—*if* it happened. She owed it to Tim to do whatever she could.

In the hall outside the sixth-grade class, Jeri doublechecked her striped pants and berry cardigan. Rosa smoothed her long-sleeved, lace-bottomed tee, tossed her waist-length hair over her shoulders, and swept into the room ahead of her. Jeri sighed. No matter how she looked, it was like Rosa was in color while she was in black and white.

She trailed behind Rosa into the brightly lit room. While taking off her jacket, and without being obvious, she glanced around the room to see who was there. *Yes!* Dallas was at a back table, talking to Jonathan Fielding. She took a seat at the table across the room.

"Settle down, people," Mr. Jenkins said. "Now that the girls' school is represented, let's get started. Isn't Abby with you?"

Jeri shook her head. "She's in the hospital." A chorus of "What?" and "What'd she say?" erupted. Jeri raised her voice. "On Thursday there was an explosion and fire in the biology lab. Abby breathed in a lot of smoke, and they took her in an ambulance." She felt Dallas's eyes on her, but she stared straight ahead. "She came home Friday, but yesterday she got sick again and went back to the hospital. She might come home today."

"She must have been seriously hurt!" Mr. Jenkins said.

Jeri nodded. "She had the flu all last week too. I think she was already weak before the fire."

"I'll call her this afternoon—maybe she'd like a visitor if she's still there. We'll certainly be praying for her." Mr. Jenkins wrote her name on the whiteboard. "What other prayer requests?"

After listing several more, they took turns praying. Jeri smiled inwardly as she listened to Dallas pray for Abby. Jeri felt uncomfortable praying out loud in class, but Dallas never sounded awkward. He said he intended to run a ranch someday, but Jeri thought he'd make a great pastor.

After class, Jeri's heart skipped a beat when she saw Dallas working his way toward her.

"I sure hope Abby gets better," he said. "Tell her we missed her."

"I will." Jeri grabbed her Bible and jacket. She, Dallas, and Rosa walked out together, heading toward the sanctuary with the rest of their class.

"See ya in there," Rosa said, stopping off at the ladies' room. "Save me a place."

"Okay." Jeri got a drink from the water fountain. When she turned around, she was surprised to find Dallas waiting for her.

"Can I ask you something?" he said.

"Sure." Jeri held her breath. Would he ask her to the dance? He didn't look nervous or anything. He probably just wanted to borrow a pen. "What?" she prompted, amazed how casual she sounded, given the flutterings in her stomach.

"Are you going to the luau next weekend?" he asked.

Her heart skipped a beat. Then another one. *Here it comes!* "I'm planning to."

"Oh, good. You want a partner for the races?"

Jeri's heart sank. "Um, well ..."

"You like to run, right? I heard you were going out for track next month."

"I am." She groaned inwardly. "I already told someone I'd be his partner for the three-legged races though."

"That's okay." Dallas' crooked smile deepened one dimple. "Guess I should have asked sooner. I'll see you there then. And no offense, but hopefully I'll beat you."

Jeri sighed and watched him join Jonathan at the activities bulletin board. He didn't seem the least bit disappointed that she'd turned him down. Or curious about who her partner was. With mixed feelings, she went into the sanctuary.

Rosa took forever joining her. The first praise and worship song was half over when she finally slid into the seat next to Jeri. "Sorry," she whispered. "I got stuck talking to Dallas."

Jeri felt her stomach clench. "What'd he want?"

"He needed a partner for the races at the luau. I warned him I'm not athletic, and we'll probably come in last."

Grateful that it was time to pray, Jeri was spared having to answer. She was so tempted to tell Rosa that Dallas had asked *her* first. Rosa probably wouldn't even care. During the rest of the service, Jeri stood and sang at all the right times, then sat and pretended to listen. If someone had offered her a hundred dollars afterwards for a summary of the sermon, she couldn't have given one. She concentrated instead on breathing around the huge lump in her throat and trying not to cry.

She'd had to turn down Dallas's invitation—and he'd asked Rosa! And her roommate was going with him! How could she?

True, Rosa didn't know how she felt about Dallas. It was the only thing all year that she *hadn't* told Rosa. She just couldn't. Rosa had so many friends that Jeri didn't think she'd understand. And she couldn't run the risk of Rosa—in her effort to help—marching right up to Dallas and telling him Jeri liked him. She'd die!

Oh *why* had she felt so sorry for Tim that she'd agreed to be his partner at the luau? She'd been waiting all year for Dallas to single her out. Now that he had—even just as a friend—she'd had to say no! The worst part was he hadn't even seemed to care. He'd substituted Rosa for her with no trouble at all.

Jeri was thankful to have a whole hour before facing Rosa on the ride home. By the time church was over, her feelings had settled down some. She kept waiting for Rosa to mention Dallas, but she never did. Jeri finally realized it was no big deal to her. It was like she'd already forgotten about it.

That afternoon, Rosa enlisted Nikki's help to work on papier-mâché palm tree decorations in the study room downstairs. Up in their room, Jeri composed a special news bulletin asking for eyewitnesses. When finished, she ran downstairs to hand her friends copies. She had to step over boxes of candles and four-inch clay pots in the shape of pineapples. "What do you think?" Jeri asked. "If the media lab was open today, I'd run off more copies now and hand them out."

Nikki draped another gloppy strip of newspaper over a wire form. "Email me the file. I'll print you enough copies to give out."

"Really? Thanks! I'll email it now."

Within an hour, Jeri had sixty copies ready to hand out. She, Nikki, and Rosa stood in the front hallway, each holding twenty. "Let's split up the area—"

Suddenly the front door opened. "Can I come in?"

"Abby, you're back!" Jeri cried.

"We just got here. Miss Barbara's parking the car." Her voice sounded lower, still kind of scratchy.

"Does it hurt to talk?" Jeri asked.

"Not too much." She hung her jacket on the hall tree. "What's going on here?"

Jeri handed her a paper. "This is a special edition. Did you hear about yesterday's fire?"

Abby nodded. "Miss Barbara said no one got hurt this time though."

"Not in the fire," Jeri said, "but Tim got accused—falsely, I think. He was seen running away from the shed. And then Mr. Rankin heard me ask him about it and said he'd get Tim fired." She sighed. "I feel so *rotten* about that."

Abby quickly read the article. "This is good. The sooner your papers get out, the sooner someone will come forward."

"Exactly." Jeri hesitated. "I hate to leave when you just got back …"

"Don't worry about it. I promised Miss Barbara I'd grab a kip right away."

"Aren't you sick of sleeping?" Rosa asked.

"Kind of, but there were tons of interruptions in the hospital. I'm wiped out. Neither one of us got much sleep." Abby hugged them each quickly and then headed upstairs. "Thanks for your cards, mates," she called over her shoulder. "And your prayers."

"Just get better." Jeri grabbed her stack of papers,

leaving some in the living room for the girls in her own house. Then Nikki and Rosa followed her outside, closing the door behind them.

Within forty-five minutes, all sixty papers were handed out. Each girl in Hampton House got one. Jeri gave Lyndsey ten papers to hand out to the girls in McClellan. Rosa headed off to post papers in the lounges of the other dorms. Nikki's job was to thumbtack papers to the bulletin boards in the library, dining hall, sports center, and theater lobby.

There, Jeri thought as she headed back to the dorm, *that should get someone's attention.*

Rosa and Nikki were already playing a game of Catch Phrase in the lounge with Mariah and Kelli. Jeri started upstairs to check on Abby when Mariah called out.

"Hey, Jeri, I saw your paper. I want to report something!"

"Really?" Jeri ran back down the stairs. "What?"

"Looks like you're trying to get your boyfriend off the hook."

Nikki shoved Mariah on the shoulder. "Cut it out."

"I'm just reporting what I see!" Mariah grinned. "His stuffed Easter bunny was too sweet. I understand why you don't want him going to juvie jail."

Heat crawled up Jeri's neck and face, setting her cheeks on fire. No one really believed Tim was her boyfriend. Or ... did they? She turned and raced upstairs, anxious to talk to Abby about it. Maybe she'd tell her what happened that morning with Dallas too. It had been sitting heavily on her mind all afternoon. Abby always listened—and most importantly, kept stuff to herself.

Jeri tapped lightly on Abby's door. When there was no answer, she opened it several inches. Abby was still napping. The shades were down, and Nikki's globe lamp gave off the only light in the room. Abby must have gone to sleep right after they left.

Disappointed, Jeri pulled the door softly closed. She guessed her problems could wait till tomorrow. They'd have to.

8
RACE TO THE FINISH

Jeri bit her lip. She ought to go back downstairs.
She couldn't investigate the fires by hiding in her room.
She pulled her shoulders back. If it meant being teased
about Tim, she'd just have to endure it.

Thankfully, when she got downstairs, their game
was over and Mariah had left. Jeri joined the girls who
were sitting around the fireplace. Pen in hand, she asked
the group if anyone knew *anything* that might help her.
While Kelli was putting the game away, she said that
she'd heard Mr. Rankin had a jail record. Maybe it was
for arson. Jeri made a note to find out—or tell the fire
marshal to check on it. Then Leah suggested that the
school needed money and maybe someone was torching
buildings so they could collect the insurance. That made
sense to Jeri. She'd mention that too.

"And I saw the security guard near the shed before the fire broke out," a girl named Mia said.

"Really? What time?" Jeri asked.

"I'm not sure." Mia wrinkled her nose. "Just before lunch, I think."

Hmmm. He'd told Jeri his shift ended at ten. If so, what was he doing around the shed at noon? Since he had keys to all the buildings, making rounds gave him an excuse to be wherever he wanted. Jeri wrote down everything they said.

On Monday morning, since Abby had been ordered to take one more day in bed, Jeri trudged alone across campus to breakfast, wishing the sun would come out. The overcast sky matched her spirits today. When she spotted The Head at the top of the dining-hall steps, she asked about Tim.

"He's suspended from working here," the headmistress said gravely, "until we get to the bottom of who's setting the fires."

"Is he suspended from helping at the luau too?"

The Head frowned. "I'll have to think about that." She cleared her throat. "You might want to ask yourself if *you* bear any responsibility if Tim is our arsonist."

"Me?" Jeri swallowed hard. "How could I be blamed for that?"

"Your newspaper article about Lyndsey. Don't you suppose you gave Tim—or someone else—the idea that setting fires would make them a celebrity?"

"That's not why I did it!"

"I realize that, but if you had checked with me or the fire marshal, we could have warned you about the dangers of copycat arsonists."

"I'm sorry," Jeri barely whispered.

As she picked up her breakfast, Jeri felt a ten-ton weight pressing down on her. Suddenly the waffles—one of her favorite breakfasts—weren't so appetizing. Over breakfast, the girls at her table talked about just two things: the fires and the luau on Saturday night.

Talk about the fire reminded Jeri that she'd cost Tim his job. If Tim didn't get to come to the luau, *that* would be her fault too. Talk about the luau sank her mood even further, as she imagined Dallas and Rosa laughing together while she tripped clumsily along in a three-legged race with Tim.

Stop it! she scolded herself. *You're making yourself miserable.* They were all friends, and Rosa had had no idea how Jeri felt about Dallas, or she wouldn't have agreed to be his partner. Jeri knew that, and yet she couldn't help the jealousy that kept popping up. For weeks Jeri had looked forward to the luau. Now, with it only five days away, she dreaded it.

After breakfast, she was scheduled to go to the library because the biology lab was still being repaired. There she picked up her book on hold and finished her math in half an hour. Now what? *I wish I could call Mom and talk.* Jeri glanced at the row of computers near the window. Two were empty. Grabbing her bag, she decided to email Mom. It was better than nothing.

In a long message, she poured out everything about Tim, the stuffed bunny, the ridicule, and having to turn Dallas down for the races. She clicked send, knowing her email was a jumbled mess, but feeling lighter for having dumped the load on Mom.

While she had the computer, Jeri remembered Mr. Rankin. Could she check him out online and see if he had a criminal record? A quick search brought up several private investigation agencies. The least expensive report cost thirty dollars, payable by credit card. She slumped back in her chair. So much for that idea.

Well, she'd research stuff about arson instead. There must be arsonist profiles or descriptions somewhere. Maybe it'd give her an idea or remind her of someone. She wasn't any fire investigator, but she knew people that the fire marshal didn't.

What she found shocked her. According to the FBI, half the people arrested for setting fires were younger than eighteen. And kids who set fires resulting in property damage or injury could be arrested for arson. According to one article, most arsonists had mental and social problems. They would continue to set fires until their problems were healed.

Jeri sat back with a feeling of foreboding. The description of a typical juvenile arsonist sounded disturbingly like Tim. Mentally and socially, he was way behind other guys his age. He was often treated like a social outcast, which had to be lonely and painful.

While mulling that over, she checked her email again before logging off. She already had a response from Mom.

Hi, Sweetie! You caught me doing homework for that online class I'm taking. I'm sorry to hear about everything you told me. I hope Abby is better today. I'll call this week. What's a good night? Love and hugs, Mom

On an impulse, Jeri sent an instant message, hoping Mom was still online.

JerichoGirl: ANY–1 HERE?

She sat and waited thirty seconds, just in case. Then a reply popped up.

imHis: Hey there, Sweetie! I was studying. I'm going to ace this test.

JerichoGirl: WTG

imHis: What? Your mom needs plain English.

JerichoGirl: ok. way to go. wish U were here. what should i do about Tim????????

imHis: I'm glad you're being his friend, even though you had to say no to Dallas. Did you agree to be Tim's partner because you felt sorry for him?

JerichoGirl: i guess. is that wrong?????????

imHis: Would you want someone to go with you because he felt sorry for you? Tim needs your genuine acceptance and caring—but not your pity.

JerichoGirl: i'm just trying 2 B nice 2 him.

imHis: That doesn't mean you can't have special

friends or that you can't be involved with certain people more than others. We shouldn't treat some people with kindness and be uncaring to others.

JerichoGirl: what do i do?????????????? Tim is hard 2 say no 2—he gets his feelings hurt.

imHis: I love that you're considering Tim's feelings. Keep your word about the three-legged race, but also do other things with Rosa or Dallas or Abby. Don't wrongly give Tim the idea that you're his girlfriend. You'd just hurt him more later, and that isn't kind.

JerichoGirl: ok. thanx mom. wanna talk friday??

imHis: That works. Gotta get back to work. I MIGHT have a surprise for you.

And she was gone. Jeri wondered about the surprise, but her thoughts were interrupted by the bell. She grabbed her books for her second-period class.

The rest of the week passed quickly and quietly. The biology lab was cleaned up, and the windows were replaced and ready for use by Wednesday. Sometimes Jeri felt guilty that she was enjoying Tim's absence, especially since it was her fault he couldn't work. All the talk now—between classes, at meals, and in the dorm at night—was about the Hawaiian luau on Saturday. Abby was back in class, Lyndsey's arm was healing, and girls had stopped asking her about her "honey bunny."

But Jeri couldn't forget what she'd read online about arsonists. They had deep psychological problems that would get worse unless treated. They tended to set fires until their "cry for help" was heard—or they were caught. According to the professionals, the arsonist would strike again. And this time it could be deadly.

On Friday night, Jeri's mom called. "What's the surprise?" Jeri asked right away.

Mom laughed. "Hello to you too. You sound better—I'm glad." She paused. "My boss—you remember Carol—is sending me to Virginia to see a client. I can time it to be in Landmark Hills Easter weekend!"

"Awesome!" Jeri hadn't seen Mom since Christmas break. "How long can you stay?"

"Overnight two nights. I'll start back right after church Easter morning."

"This is the best surprise," Jeri said. *Hmmm ... Church on Easter*. Maybe she could introduce Mom to Dallas.

On Saturday morning, Jeri thanked God for the gorgeous weather after the blustery week. She, Nikki, and Abby had agreed to help on Rosa's decorating committee. Jeri put the fires out of her mind as they all rode in Ms. Carter's car to Gracey Park. When they arrived, girls from Landmark's middle school and high school were already transforming the plain white shelter house into the setting for a Hawaiian luau party.

Rosa turned in a slow circle. "We'll put the coconuts and wax fruit over there. And the candles floating in pineapple pots go on that ledge around the dance floor," she said, pointing above. "We'll add the water later."

A CD of tropical island music played while they worked. Some older girls put colorful stuffed parrots in the tall inflatable palm trees outside the shelter house. Then they grouped some pink flamingos, balanced on one leg, around the entrance. Jeri spotted Lyndsey helping hang strings of electric tiki lights around the shelter house and yelled "hi!"

Beside the door, a tall surfboard was stuck in the ground, with ALOHA painted across it in neon green. Wind chimes hung in the trees, and a wooden totem pole marked the direction to the games. Jeri loved watching the park's transformation. Inside the shelter house, colorful paper lanterns hung from the rafters. On the walls, travel posters depicting various Hawaiian islands were interspersed with movie posters of *Gidget Goes Hawaiian* and an Elvis movie called *Blue Hawaii.*

The shelter house was filled with round tables sporting grass table skirts; the tables would be removed later for the dance. Table centerpieces consisted of shells, colorful paper leis, and wax fruit. Multicolored helium-balloon fish dipped and swayed when a breeze blew through.

Jeri gave Rosa a high five as they surveyed the decorations. "Your committee really outdid itself. You'd think we were on some island."

"That's the idea." Rosa smiled. "I bet Dallas will like it too."

Jeri's smile faded, and she said nothing. Yes, for sure, Dallas would love it.

They spent the afternoon back at the dorm, fighting
for the showers, practicing last-minute hula steps and
backbends for the limbo, and then dressing in their luau
costumes. Rosa had bought a grass skirt to wear over her
shorts, huge sunglasses, a shell necklace, a floppy beach
hat, and sequined flip-flops.

"Look!" she said, plopping the hat on top of her long
curls and twirling around the room.

Jeri fought the envy that rose in her. Rosa looked so
cute that she'd have every boy at the dance fighting to
be her partner. Jeri glanced down. With her cut-off shorts,
flowered shirt, and paper lei, she looked like 90 percent of
the girls going. When Nikki appeared in their doorway,
she was wearing the same outfit she wore every weekend:
her leather boots, denim jeans, and a denim shirt. For the
luau, she'd stuck a paper flower in her hair, but it hung
upside down over one ear.

At three thirty, they lined up outside to ride buses over
to the park. When they arrived, none of the boys were
there yet. Rosa and Nikki went to help with food. Jeri and
Abby strolled down the center of the park, where the boys
had set up various booths after lunch.

"Look at that," Abby said, pointing.

The boys had set up a game called "hot coconut" that
was like hot potato with tropical music. Next, there was a
coconut bowling game, where players were challenged to
get a spare or strike by knocking down plastic pineapples.

The "hula-hoop spin-off" promised big prizes for the person who kept his or her hoop spinning the longest. Near the edge of Sutter Lake was a place to fish for "sharks." At the bottom of several wading pools menacing-looking plastic sharks lurked. Rows of fishing poles stood ready nearby.

As she and Abby strolled around the magically transformed park, Jeri found herself getting excited about the luau despite being Tim's partner. After all, it was only one three-legged race. She was making a big deal out of nothing. Still tired from her time in the hospital, Abby decided to rest under a tree while Jeri walked down to the lake.

A few minutes later, Mariah gave Jeri's lei a jerk as she ran by. "Your boyfriend's here!"

Turning, Jeri spotted Tim, dressed in a flowered blue shirt, climbing out of a green car in the parking lot. He waved as the car pulled away. Apparently The Head hadn't barred him from the luau after all. Jeri's good intentions evaporated like fog on a sunny morning. *I'm not ready for this,* she thought.

Doing an about-face, she hiked with long strides to the shelter house, heading directly for the restroom. Inside, she leaned against the sink. *God, why do people have to be so mean when I'm only trying to be nice?* She didn't admire herself for it, but she cared what others thought. She didn't want everyone at both schools to think she was Tim's girlfriend. Why did loving or accepting others have to be so complicated?

She splashed her face with water and stared at her reflection. Taking a deep breath, she said, "Stop being such a chicken."

Just then, Nikki popped into the restroom, the front of her shirt covered with juicy mashed strawberries.

"What happened to you?" Jeri asked.

"Blender went berserk. I was helping to make smoothies." She wetted some paper towels and scrubbed at her shirt, smearing the stain even worse. "Tim's looking for you. Why are you hiding in here?"

"I'm not hiding!" Jeri said, stung by the truth.

"Sure you are. I saw your face earlier. You couldn't get in here fast enough."

Jeri sighed. "I can't avoid him forever," she said. "We're signed up for the three-legged race together."

"You sound like that creepy Lisa Poole." Nikki cocked her head to one side. "You care what others think as much as she does."

"No, I don't!"

"Oh yeah? Why were you so friendly to Tim in the first place?"

"What?" Jeri frowned. "What do you mean?"

"Didn't you just want people to think you're such a great Christian?"

Jeri stepped back. "That's mean."

"Pretending to be Tim's friend and then hiding from him in the bathroom is meaner."

"You're wrong. I don't care what anyone else thinks."
Jeri only cared what God thought, but since Nikki wasn't a
Christian, she'd never understand that.

Nikki studied her from head to toe, one eyebrow raised
as if she could read Jeri's mind.

Jeri felt her face heat up. Was that really why she was
trying to be nice to Tim? She knew she was only supposed
to be concerned with what God thought. The truth was that
she cared what the others—including Dallas—thought
about her. She knew believers were recognized as followers
of Jesus by the love shown to one another—but sometimes
it was so hard to do what you were supposed to do.

"Tim just needs a friend." Nikki rinsed her shirt. "If you
really don't care what those girls think, go out there and
prove it."

Face flaming hot, Jeri pushed past Nikki to leave. She
looked for Tim, but didn't see him. She felt like crying when
she spotted Rosa with Dallas at the coconut bowling. She
couldn't find Abby in the crowd, but Lyndsey was helping
set out food on long tables decorated with miniature flip-
flops and children's sunglasses. At any other time, the
smells of barbequed chicken and coconut cake would have
made her mouth water.

For the next ten minutes, Jeri wandered through the
crowd in the park. She very carefully did *not* look for Dallas
or Rosa. She was determined to have fun.

"Jeri! I found you!"

Jeri cringed at the sound of Tim's high-pitched voice
behind her. Then she shot up a quick prayer. *If you love*

me, you'll obey me. "Hi, Tim," she said, putting on a smile before turning around. "Isn't this a cool party?"

"It's almost time for the three-legged race. You ready?"

As ready as I'll ever be, Jeri thought. "You bet!" she said, ignoring someone's snicker behind her. "We'll beat everybody."

"Come on!" Tim said, pulling on Jeri's arm.

There were two races, and they would be running in the first one for the middle school grades. A rope of tiki lights tied between two trees was the starting line, and kids milled around behind it. Down the row, Dallas caught her eye and waved. "See ya at the finish line!" he yelled.

Jeri smiled, but Dallas had already turned back to Rosa. She groaned when she spotted Miss Barbara with a video camera at the finish line. She did *not* want this recorded for anyone to ever see again.

Each racing pair was given a long string cut from a grass skirt. "Stand side by side, facing the finish line by the shelter house," said a deep voice over the loudspeaker. "Tie your inside legs together at the ankle, using your string. You must stay tied together the whole race, and you must use all three 'legs' to walk or run to the finish line. Otherwise you're disqualified. People always think this race looks easy—until they try it. Teamwork is the key."

Laughter broke out as pairs of students tied their ankles together. Tim tried, but kept bumping into Jeri and falling over. The other pairs were tied together and waiting on them when Abby ran up to help.

"Let me do it," she said, smiling. "Tim, stand tall beside Jeri."

"Okay." He jammed his baseball cap down on his head and wrapped his arm around Jeri's waist.

"*Ooohh!*" several kids behind her said.

Jeri's face blazed, and she removed Tim's arm. "I keep my balance better if I'm free to move." Finally they were tied securely together.

The announcer said, "The first four pairs to cross that finish line will get a prize." He blew a whistle, and the chatter died down. "On your mark. Get set." *Tweeeeet!*

The pairs on each side of them took off. Glancing left, Jeri spotted Rosa and Dallas moving forward in perfect coordination. They'd win at that rate. She and Tim took only two steps before he tripped her, and they both went down. Jeri banged her knee on the hard ground, and Tim's elbow gouged her in the ribs.

"Get up!" she yelled over the screaming on the sidelines.

They crawled to their feet and half-jerked, half-stumbled five more steps before going down again. By the time they struggled to their feet once more, a huge cheer went up at the finish line.

The race was over. They'd been left in the dust.

Several girls and guys were pointing at them and laughing. Jeri felt as humiliated as she'd known she would. Bending to untie their string, she became aware of other voices. Nikki and Abby whistled and cheered. Nikki stared at Jeri, challenging her. Jeri gazed back.

Prove it, Nikki had said earlier. *If you really don't care what those girls think, prove it.* Jeri knew she couldn't do it on her own though. *Help me, God, to show your love to him.*

Jeri glanced at Tim, whose big eyes had filled with tears. Yes, people looked at Tim's outward appearance, which wasn't at all appealing by the world's standards. But God looked at his heart—and Jeri knew that Tim's kind and tender heart was all that mattered. In a split second, she made her decision.

"Great job, partner," she said, shaking Tim's hand. "We fell with more style than anybody else here."

"We did?" Tim looked puzzled and wiped away his tears. "Aren't you mad?"

"Why would I be mad?" Jeri adjusted the lei that had slipped behind her neck. "We came to have a good time, and I'm having a great time. What's next?"

Tim's face broke into a huge smile. "Wanna catch a shark?"

"Me too?" Abby said.

Nikki stood behind her and nodded, giving Jeri a slow smile. "Count me in."

The rest of the afternoon's games were fun. At the hoola-hoop spin-off, Jeri managed to keep her hoop spinning long enough to win a plastic flamingo pin. She handed it to Tim. Grinning, he proudly pinned it to the front of his ball cap.

And when Jeri turned around, she smacked right into Dallas.

9
DYNAMITE DANCE

"Whoa!" Dallas said, catching Jeri before she fell.

"Sorry!" Jeri backed up, stepped on Tim's foot, and stumbled. Regaining her footing, she glanced up in mortification and gave Dallas a sheepish grin.

Thankfully Rosa was nowhere around. Abby pointed at the shelter house. "We'll go save a table," she said, and she and Nikki headed toward the coconut cake aroma.

"How's your day going?" Dallas asked.

"It's been a lot of fun. I hope we do it every year." Jeri smiled up at Tim. "Tim, this is Dallas. We go to the same church. Dallas, this is Tim. He works at our school."

"Hi, Tim. I like your cap."

Tim showed Dallas all the buttons as they meandered over to the shelter house. "Want to sit with us girls?" Jeri asked. Both boys nodded, and they quickly filled the six chairs.

Half an hour later, Jeri felt too stuffed to move, but it was time to turn the shelter house into a dance floor. Darkness had fallen while they ate, and the breeze coming off Sutter Lake raised goose bumps on her arms. Rosa's pineapple pots with the floating candles set just the right mood.

While moving chairs to the edge of the dance floor, Jeri watched Tim and Dallas loading pickup trucks with folded tables to take back to Landmark. Tim was a head taller than Dallas—and a good forty pounds heavier—but they worked well side by side.

Sudden shouts erupted near one of the trucks in the parking lot. Jeri went outside to see what the commotion was about. Two older boys were shoving Tim, and he'd dropped his end of the table. One yelled, "Whatcha gonna set on fire tonight?"

"Oh no," Jeri muttered under her breath, digging her fingernails into the rough bark of a tree.

The security guard raced toward the parking lot, but before he got there, an amazing thing happened. Dallas stepped between Tim and the hecklers, saying something Jeri couldn't hear. Then he stood perfectly still in the pool of light from the street lamp, staring at the older boys until they finally turned and shuffled away. He slapped Tim on the back, and then they continued loading tables.

When they were finishing, a car slid to the curb and honked. "I'm coming!" Tim yelled. He lifted the last table onto the truck, shook Dallas's hand, and then ran awkwardly toward the car and climbed in. As they drove away, he leaned out the car window and waved.

Dallas hiked up the hill to the shelter house, and Jeri waited for him on a bench. "Thanks for what you did down there," she said, batting a green fish-shaped balloon. "Kids give Tim a hard time."

"Do people really think he's the arsonist?" Dallas asked.

"Some do. I don't." She glanced inside the shelter house where Rosa and Lyndsey were practicing the limbo. "I'll tell you about it sometime. If you want, that is."

"I do." Dallas inclined his head toward the dance floor. "You gonna try that?"

Jeri took a deep breath. "I'm not much good, but I'm working at not caring what other people think." She grinned suddenly. "During the limbo would be a good time to practice humility."

Dallas laughed, and Jeri loved the sound of it. "Think you could teach me how to bend over backward like that?" he asked.

"Sure." She jumped up and brushed sand from her shorts. "Come on."

They joined Rosa and Lyndsey in line to go under the limbo bar, while Abby snapped photos and Nikki ran

Hampton House's video recorder. Beach Boys music blared over two loudspeakers, and kids on the sidelines stomped and cheered each time the limbo bar was lowered. Half an hour later, Jeri collapsed, exhausted and happy, onto a chair at the edge of the dance floor. When was the last time she'd had so much fun? She couldn't remember.

"Want some soda?" Dallas asked, leaning against the wooden railing beside her.

"Sure. Thanks." He and two friends went to stand in the refreshment line.

Jeri leaned her head back and closed her eyes, absorbing the music and the laughter around her. As she breathed deeply and her pulse slowed, she became aware of an odd odor when the breeze blew her way. What was it? She sat up and sniffed, looked around, and sniffed again.

Finally she glanced up at the candle on the ledge above her head. She stood up, raised up on her tiptoes, and peered inside the four-inch clay pineapple pot. It was half filled with water with a yellow candle floating in it. She frowned and then sniffed. That wasn't water.

It smelled like *alcohol*.

Someone had emptied the water from this candle holder and replaced it with alcohol. And alcohol was flammable!

Sweat broke out on Jeri's forehead and neck. The candle was half burned down already. When the flame hit the liquid, it wouldn't go out like the other candles. Instead, there'd be an explosion big enough to blow off someone's hand—and burn down the shelter house.

Jeri looked around frantically. Should she try to blow it out now? Or would that push the flame so close to the alcohol that it would ignite in her face? If she didn't do something *now*, though, the fumes could ignite anyway.

Just then Dallas came back alone, holding out a red cup. "Root beer. It's all they had."

"It's perfect," she said, grabbing it fast.

She moved to dump the root beer on the flame, but then pulled back. Would liquid splash the flame down into the alcohol? She couldn't take that chance. She dipped her fingers into the root beer and lifted them, dripping, to the candle.

"What are you doing?" Dallas asked.

Reaching down inside, Jeri pressed her wet fingers and thumb together over the wick. With a hiss, the flame went out.

Jeri collapsed hard on the folding chair, her heart thudding. Sweat ran down between her shoulder blades.

"What's wrong?" Dallas demanded.

"Smell the candle."

He sniffed. "Kerosene?" he asked. "Alcohol?"

Jeri nodded. "A bomb waiting to go off. Someone replaced the water with alcohol." She glanced around the shelter house. Her eyes widened in fright. "Dallas, all those candles!"

He pulled her to her feet. "Go tell your headmistress while I check the other candles. Hurry!"

Jeri pushed through the crowd of dancing kids to Ms. Carter, who was chatting with Miss Barbara and The Head behind the refreshments table. She quickly explained what she'd found, and the three women spread out rapidly to check the remaining candles. One other pot was filled with alcohol. The rest were only water.

Jeri shivered, more from barely averting disaster than from the chilly breeze. Across the room, Abby and Nikki were watching with raised eyebrows, but Jeri just shook her head. She'd explain later.

Shuddering, Jeri glanced at Dallas, and she knew from the look on his face that his thoughts matched hers. Who might have been hurt—or killed—if they hadn't spotted the time bombs? They'd outsmarted the arsonist tonight, by the grace of God. But when would he—or she—strike again?

The Head leaned close to Jeri to be heard over the music. "An explosion tonight could have injured dozens of students. Thank you for your sharp eyes and quick thinking." She shook her head. "I guess this clinches it. Just like the other times, Tim left the scene and was out of danger before the explosions and fire were supposed to occur."

Jeri glanced at Dallas and took a deep breath. "I understand why Tim is suspended until the arsonist is caught, but I don't believe he started any fires."

The Head fingered the flower lei around her neck. "Facts are facts, Jeri. The fire marshal found a button from Tim's cap in the wastebasket in the biology lab. Tim admitted it's his." Her scowl looked set in stone. "Tim was in that lab, no matter what he said otherwise. And he was in the shed just before it burned. And he was here tonight!"

Jeri frowned. That button probably fell off his hat into the water bucket while he was mopping. Then Lyndsey dumped it in the wastebasket herself when she doused the flames. "It could have—"

But The Head had turned and stalked off without another word.

"I have to go too," Dallas said. "Let's talk at Sunday school tomorrow, okay?"

Jeri nodded. "Just keep praying," she said. Outside the shelter house, she leaned against a rough-barked tree. Soon the music stopped, and boys from Patterson headed to the parking lot to board their buses.

On the way home fifteen minutes later, while girls all around her chattered a mile a minute, Jeri leaned her hot forehead against the cool bus window. Was The Head right? Was it obvious to everyone but her that Tim had started the fires?

If that was true—if he *was* the arsonist—how could she stop him before someone got killed?

10
TRAPPED!

Jeri was anxious to talk to Dallas after Sunday school the next morning, so she was doubly disappointed when he wasn't there. The van from the boys' school didn't show up at all. At the end of class, Mr. Jenkins got a call on his cell phone. Apparently their van had broken down.

Nikki was waiting for Jeri when she got back from church. "You busy this afternoon?" she asked. "I need someone to videotape me after lunch. I want to watch my performance and see where I can improve."

"Do you have a video camera?"

"Ms. Carter said I can use this one." She held up the small camcorder belonging to Hampton House.

"I guess I can do that."

After lunch, Jeri checked her email and found something that brought a smile to her face. Dallas had written to her.

> *Had a good time at the luau. I liked how nice you were to Tim. I'm praying for him. You're different from most girls. See you next Sunday!*

An hour later, Rosa and Abby left with a group to clean up the luau decorations at the park. Still lighthearted over Dallas's email, Jeri followed Nikki across campus. It was overcast again, but at least it wasn't raining. *I'd give anything for two sunny days in a row,* she thought.

She practiced with the video camera a few minutes while Nikki saddled up.

"I'll warm up first," Nikki said. She walked Show Stopper, and then trotted and cantered around the indoor riding ring six or seven times. Leaning against the fence, Jeri inhaled the smell of sawdust and let her mind finally relax as she watched Nikki's perfect rhythm. No wonder she loved riding so much. *If I could ride like that, I'd live in this barn too.*

Nikki reined in beside Jeri. "You ready?"

"Yup. What should I tape?"

"Start now, and just keep it running till I yell. If you stand on that crate, you'll get a better angle."

"Okay." Jeri climbed up. "Ready."

For the next twenty minutes, Jeri taped as Nikki put Show Stopper through his paces. It truly was like watching a horse ballet, Jeri thought, as she tried to hold the camera steady. The way Show Stopper lifted his front legs so high while balancing on his massive hind quarters was breathtaking to watch.

"Cut!" Nikki called as she trotted up to Jeri. "That should do it."

"You going back now?" Jeri asked, jumping down.

"No, that last part was rough. We'll run through it a few times and then cool down. Just leave the camera there."

"Okay. *Adiós!*"

For a few minutes Jeri walked aimlessly through the Equestrian Center. She saw three girls leaving on a trail ride and two more in the outdoor practice ring. If only she had something to do. She wouldn't even mind hanging out with Tim. She'd go back to the dorm, but Rosa and Abby wouldn't be back yet.

She stopped outside Prancer's stall. "Hi, boy," she said, reaching out for him to nuzzle her palm. "Looks like you got clean straw yesterday."

She grabbed a bucket of brushes and picks off a nail outside the door. Something about the smell of the barn—the horses, the leather, the hay, even the manure—was so peaceful. She slipped into his stall and picked up a comb to work the knots out of his mane and tail. He snuffled and snorted and stamped his feet.

"What's the matter?" Jeri asked, stroking his neck. "Settle down."

He whinnied and stamped his feet some more instead.

Scrambling movements overhead made her think first of mice, but it was louder than that. She stopped and listened hard. Then she grinned. *The kittens!* She bet that's where the pregnant Loretta had gone to have her babies.

Suddenly Prancer's ears lay back, and he snorted and shied, bumping into her. "Whoa there," Jeri crooned, getting alarmed herself. "What's with you?" Prancer's wild eyes were rolled back with the whites showing, and he danced sideways.

Then Jeri smelled it: smoke!

She ran out of the stall and looked overhead to the open loft. Wisps of smoke were rising from the bales of hay above. She scrambled up the splintery board ladder nailed to the side of the wall. Up in the dark, dusty loft, she peered into the gloom and spotted a figure in the far corner. Smoke rose behind her.

"Lyndsey? What are *you* doing up here?"

When she didn't answer, Jeri jumped around her and got behind the bales to stamp on the flickering flames in the hay. They licked at the dry straw and spread faster than she could stamp it out.

"Help me!" she yelled at Lyndsey.

Lyndsey sprang forward and grabbed Jeri by the shoulders. "We have to get out of here!"

"No! The horses will burn! Help me get the fire out!"

Lyndsey pulled on Jeri's arm until she fell backwards on the floor of the hayloft. Then Lyndsey dragged her over to the ladder.

Jeri pulled and tried to yank her arm loose, but Lyndsey was surprisingly strong.

What is going on? Then suddenly Jeri realized exactly what was happening. Lyndsey didn't want Jeri to put out the fires because, before Jeri arrived, Lyndsey had been up in the loft *starting* her next fire. *She* was the arsonist!

Smoke rose now from several locations in the loft, and Jeri grabbed a fistful of chaff from the floor of the loft and threw it in Lyndsey's eyes. Lyndsey yelled and released her grip for a moment. Jeri rolled sideways and scrambled on hands and knees to the corner where smoke was thickest.

Among the loose piles of hay, a small yellow ball of fire, bright as the sun, grew and roared into life. Below, Prancer and several other horses whinnied and kicked their stalls. *I have to put the fire out.*

If only the stable hand were here! But Sam never worked on Sundays. The Center was nearly deserted.

On her feet again, Jeri stomped and pounded at the flames. The smoke was thickening, and Jeri's eyes watered. She turned and saw through the haze that Lyndsey was descending the ladder.

Jeri coughed and struggled to breathe. The fire was getting away from her. She had to get help.

She scrambled to the ladder and started down. Lyndsey was already nowhere to be seen. Racing against time, Jeri's foot slipped on the third rung from the bottom. She lost her footing and fell backwards to the cement floor below. It knocked the breath from her.

On both sides of her, horses stamped in their stalls, neighing and whinnying, some kicking the boards. Jeri kept trying to breathe, but her chest felt paralyzed. Had she broken her back? She couldn't move.

I can't breathe! Help me, God!

Suddenly she gulped in air, swallowing smoke, and coughed so hard she vomited. Lying crumpled on her side, she tried desperately to draw a breath. Overhead, straw burned brightly, and hay made thick rolling smoke.

She crawled painfully to her feet and nearly buckled. She must have sprained her ankle in the fall. Through the smoke she glimpsed Lyndsey running down the aisle, letting the frantic, screaming horses loose. One after another, she aimed them toward the open barn door and slapped their backs hard. *Heroic Lyndsey to the rescue again*, Jeri thought.

Suddenly it was so clear. Lyndsey had started the lab fire, then run to rescue everyone. Had she planned to rescue Tim at the shed too, only he'd run away scared? She'd definitely started the barn fire. Who was going to be blamed for *this* fire while Lyndsey, the hero, saved the school's horses?

Coughing from the heavy, swirling smoke, Jeri felt the heat above her head as the flames took hold in the barn roof. The noise of screaming horses kicking stalls was deafening. Limping painfully, Jeri stumbled to the open door. Beside her, a horse panicked, reared, and headed back toward the flames, knocking Lyndsey down. He nearly stepped on her, turned again, and then ran outside through the open door.

Jeri gulped fresh air, then turned and limped back into the barn. Her raised arm shielded eyes that were blinded by the smoke. Where was Lyndsey? Was she knocked unconscious?

Jeri groped along the floor, losing her bearings in the swirling smoke. The hazy curtain threatened to choke and smother her. Crawling along the barn floor, she called Lyndsey's name.

Finally her hands touched a leg, then an arm. "Get up! Hang onto me!" Jeri yelled, helping the other girl to stand. Lyndsey leaned heavily on Jeri, and Jeri bit her lip against the ankle pain as they slowly made their way out of the burning barn.

Sparks flew. Before them and behind them, flames licked along the floor and up the walls of the stalls. Jeri stumbled blindly forward, blundering into a wall. Her face burned as she passed through the flickering fire. She felt a draft of cool air and headed blindly toward it, dragging Lyndsey with her. Coughing hard, she finally found the open barn door.

With a final lunge, they were outside. Jeri was vaguely aware of the milling horses and people and a fire engine wailing in the distance. She collapsed on the grass, pulling Lyndsey down with her. Lyndsey tried to crawl away, but Jeri held tight.

"Stop it!" Jeri shouted. "You're not going anywhere."

Summoning a last bit of strength, Jeri straddled Lyndsey's ankles. As Lyndsey struggled, her jeans skirt was pushed above her knees. Jeri stared openmouthed at Lyndsey's legs—and the ugly red burn scars that covered them.

Several more horses suddenly plunged outside through the smoky entrance, running past Jeri. Then she heard an unearthly scream coming from the barn. A human scream.

Nikki!

She must have been trapped in Show Stopper's stall! Jeri had to get her out!

But before she could make her legs work, two more people stumbled through the smoke and emerged outside. One was Nikki—and she was being carried by Tim.

An hour later Jeri, Tim, and Nikki sat under a spreading white pine tree near the Equestrian Center, their oxygen masks now in their laps. Their coughing was better, and Jeri was able to piece things together. The police and one medical technician had already taken a very subdued Lyndsey away, and the firefighters were mostly done putting out the blaze. One corner of the barn roof was gone, and charred beams showed through. Jeri guessed half the hay was burned up too.

Someone had corralled the loose horses in the outdoor riding rings. Tim had been able to free the rest of the trapped horses, including Show Stopper. Headmistress Long was kneeling in the grass—*unheard of!*—next to Jeri, Tim, and Nikki. The medical techs had gone to treat a couple firefighters, but not until all three kids were out of danger.

"I owe you a huge apology, Jeri," The Head said. "Your newspaper article didn't cause any copycat fires. And I apologize to you too, Tim. I'm afraid Lyndsey had me completely fooled. At least, until earlier today."

"What happened earlier?" Jeri asked.

"I was reading your newspaper article again about the lab fire. As I studied Lyndsey's photo, something stirred in the back of my mind. I dug into Lyndsey's family file, and what I read there set off a lot of alarms."

According to Lyndsey's records, Head Long explained, two years ago her family had a house fire. Lyndsey had tried to save her little sister, but failed. Her sister died in the fire, and Lyndsey was badly scarred.

Earlier that afternoon, after reading her file, The Head had gone to McClellan House to talk to the house mother and search Lyndsey's room. "I found several flammable liquids—mostly painting supplies. I also found three more lighters under her mattress."

While searching the room, The Head had questioned Lyndsey's roommate. Apparently Lyndsey wore long skirts and pants every evening and weekend—no matter what the weather—and dark tights with her school uniforms. She refused to take swimming lessons, and not even her roommate had ever seen her bare legs.

Jeri nodded. "She wouldn't even let the nurse in the infirmary help her get out of her wet clothes," she said, recalling the day she'd taken Lyndsey's photo. "She has burns on her forehead too, under her bangs. I thought it was a birthmark when I saw it."

The Head fingered her pearl earring. "The police officer feels Lyndsey is somehow trying to make up for not rescuing her sister. He thinks she sets fires so she gets another chance to be a hero and rescue people now." Her voice dropped. "I guess people start fires for many reasons, some of them very sad."

"And all year she pretended to have a little sister at home," Jeri said. "Lyndsey said she talked to her on the phone and did stuff with her at Christmas."

"All made up," The Head said sadly. "But you couldn't have known. Her family flies her home to Florida for vacations instead of coming here. I'm sorry I didn't believe you, Tim," Head Long said again.

"That's all right. I'm not mad." He smiled then. "Jeri believed me."

Nikki reached over and took Tim's arm. "Thank you for getting me and Show Stopper out. Where did you come from?"

"I was cleaning in the tack room while Sam was gone." He looked at The Head guiltily. "I'm sorry. I know you said to stay away, but I missed my job. I rode my bike out here." He shrugged. "I heard the horses, and then I heard someone scream. It was hard to find you in the smoke."

"And to think what might have happened ..." The Head shuddered. "I'll talk to Mr. Rankin about you immediately, Tim. Report for work tomorrow, all right?"

Tim saluted, knocking off his cap in the process. "I'll be here."

Headmistress Long stood slowly. She brushed off her skirt and then ordered the crowd of onlookers to disperse to the dorms or library for an hour. The firefighters would stick around a while to make sure the fire was totally out.

"I promised the EMTs that you all would head to the infirmary," Head Long told the trio under the tree. "If you don't go now, they'll take you to the hospital for observation. I'll be over after I talk to the police about Lyndsey." She glanced quickly at the squad car, where Lyndsey sat in the backseat. "They need to know her history. She'll need a lot of counseling for the traumatic loss in her family. She has a long, long road of recovery ahead of her."

Jeri nodded. Glancing at Tim, she realized he and Lyndsey actually had some things in common. They both had events from their pasts—ordeals that weren't their fault—that had produced within them special needs. *But how should I feel about what Lyndsey did?* Jeri wondered. Maybe the answer was the same as with Tim: *"Do unto others ..."* Tim needed love and acceptance; Lyndsey's special needs would involve a lot of forgiveness and understanding.

Dragging themselves to their feet, Jeri, Nikki, and Tim headed toward Clarke Hall, skirting around the crowd still gathered at the barn. "Well, I'm glad that's over," Jeri finally said, realizing her throat *really* felt raw this time.

She wanted to call Mom, but it would hurt to talk long enough to tell the whole story. Then she remembered the surprise.

"Mom's coming next weekend for Easter," she said. "I'd like to plan a picnic in the park for her with all my friends." She grabbed Tim's ball cap and jammed it down on her own tangled, smoky hair. "And that includes *you*."

faThGirLz!
2 corinthians 4:18

BOARDING SCHOOL MYSTERIES

PICK YOUR POISON

KRISTI HOLL

1

SNEAK ATTACK

Birthday parties were supposed to be fun, but that warm Saturday evening, nothing went as Jeri McKane expected. Illness was the last thing on her mind as a cardinal whistled outside her open window. She had no clue that in two short hours her friends would be poisoned.

Jeri twisted from side to side in front of the mirror. "What's wrong with how I look?" she asked her roommate. Her dark blue shirt complemented both her jeans and the denim flats with red bows.

"What's *wrong* with it?" Rosa Sanchez peered over her shoulder. "It looks like something your mom would wear." Rosa always looked cool—like now, in her short denim skirt and tee with a fuzzy pink scarf. Her black waist-length hair made any outfit look awesome. "Want to borrow something?" she asked with a wink. "Don't forget, Dallas is coming tonight. What if he brings some cutie with him and you look like that?"

Dallas. Jeri's heart skipped a beat, and she turned her back to Rosa to hide the blush that flooded her face. Dallas Chandler, a boy from their church, attended the Patterson School for Boys on the other side of Landmark Hills. So far, Jeri had done a good job of hiding her crush on him. She refused to risk Rosa telling Dallas about her feelings. Before Christmas, Rosa had done that to a boy Abby liked, and Abby had nearly died of shame.

"How about this?" Rosa held up a lavender top with a lace edge. Then she grabbed a short black skirt from her closet. "Or this?"

"Hmm." It was tempting, even if it was awfully short. "I suppose I could wear tights with it."

"No way, José!" Rosa shook her head. "Show off those legs!" She frowned. "You're awfully white though. You have any of that bronze gel stuff?"

"No." Jeri glanced at her watch. "Anyway, I gotta get downstairs. I'm setting tables for Abby."

Tonight, Abby Wright, the girl from England who lived in the dorm room next to theirs, was fixing a meal for eight people. It was her home ec project, and it included a birthday cake for another sixth grader who lived there in Hampton House. Since part of her grade was based on proper boy/

girl etiquette at a dinner, Dallas and a friend had agreed to show up and lend a hand.

Just then, heavy footsteps pounded up the stairs, and Jeri whipped around as their door burst open. Nikki Brown's face was beaded with sweat. "Come quick! Both of you."

"What's the matter?" Jeri asked.

"You know Abby's tuna turnovers? A tube of biscuits exploded!"

Jeri gasped. "No way!"

"It was sitting on the stove while the oven preheated."

"I saw something like that on TV," Rosa said. "Groceries were left in a car parked in the sun. It got so hot the cans of biscuits exploded all over the car."

"Exactly." Nikki rolled her eyes. "The grocery store's delivery guy is busy, so Ms. Carter's driving Abby there for more biscuits." Nikki flicked some lettuce off her fringed leather vest. "I was making the salad, but now I have to clean up the biscuit glop. I can't do everything!"

"We'll help," Jeri said. "Is the birthday cake okay?"

"Sorta. A flying biscuit mashed some of the frosting."

"I'll fix the cake." Rosa put on a pink ball cap with a silver band. "Nikki, you clean up the biscuit mess. Jeri's setting the tables."

"Okay, but hurry up. Those guys get here in half an hour." Nikki's cowboy boots clomped back down the stairs.

Jeri turned back to the mirror. Should she wear the skirt or shouldn't she? In the mirror's reflection, she spotted the desktop photo of her and her mom sitting in their porch swing back home in Iowa. Her mom's trusting smile made her hesitate. And yet, if she was old enough to go to school halfway across the country, wasn't she old enough to dress herself without Mom's advice? If only the skirt wasn't quite so short ...

Jeri handed Rosa's skirt back. "Thanks, anyway." She yanked a comb through her shoulder-length brown hair, added a headband, and followed Rosa down the steps.

"Weird to have the dorm so quiet tonight," Rosa said.

Jeri nodded. Most of the girls were eating supper in the dining hall. Miss Barbara, their assistant house mother, planned to take them roller skating afterward. Only Emily—the birthday girl—and her roommate, Brooke, were still upstairs in their room, waiting for Abby's dinner.

Downstairs, the kitchen was a disaster. Globs of sticky biscuit dough stuck to the floor, the table, the stove, and the windowsill. One biscuit had mashed a yellow frosting rose and the green *y* from *Birthday*. Rosa immediately went to work on the cake.

Nikki was on the floor scraping up pieces of canned biscuits. The makings for the turnover filling—tuna, shredded cheese, ripe olives, and hardboiled eggs—were on the counter, waiting to be mixed and wrapped inside biscuit dough. *Poor Abby!* Jeri thought as she went to set the tables and arrange flowers.

Down the hall, two card tables and eight chairs were already set up in the first-floor study room. Disposable items—bright yellow paper tablecloths, plates, and cups, plus plastic silverware—were in a sack beside the door. Jeri quickly set both tables.

Also by the door was a huge bouquet of yellow daffodils with orange centers, enough flowers for two centerpieces. She breathed deeply; she *loved* that smell. Using the sharp knife lying there, she followed Abby's written instructions to cut an inch off each stem before putting the flowers in vases.

As she worked, she allowed herself to pretend that the flowers were *hers*, and Dallas had surprised her with them. "Just to celebrate spring," he might say, giving her that slow Southern grin and a wink.

"Are you done?" Nikki called from the doorway, making her jump.

"Ow!" Jeri dropped the knife. A thin red line appeared on her thumb, and blood dripped on a daffodil. "Get me a Band-Aid, will you?"

Nikki dashed off and reappeared with the kitchen's first-aid kit. She wiped Jeri's cut and applied disinfectant cream and a Band-Aid. "You okay?" At Jeri's nod, Nikki headed back to the kitchen. Jeri finished the bouquets, tossing the stems and the bloom with her blood on it in the garbage.

In the kitchen, Jeri found things more under control. Rosa had fixed the *y* on top of the cake and removed the flattened rose. The biscuits were in the wastebasket. Nikki was breaking fresh mushrooms into small pieces for the salad, while Rosa grated a carrot to add. The filling for the turnovers still needed to be mixed.

"Should I go ahead—" Jeri was cut off as Abby and the housemother rushed in the back door.

Abby's gaze darted around the room, then she visibly relaxed. "You guys are the best mates!" She set a new can of biscuits onto the counter. "Thank you!" After shrugging off her jacket, she dumped the ingredients into a mixing bowl.

Jeri gave Abby's shoulder a quick squeeze. "Everything else is done. Can I help with the turnovers while you get dressed?"

"I wish!" Abby tucked her wind-blown blonde hair behind her ears. "I can have helpers for everything but the main dish. I have to cook it by myself."

"While I take photos for proof," Ms. Carter said, clicking away with her digital camera.

"Wait, Jer, can you do something else for me?" Abby asked, stirring her ingredients together. "Have Emily and Brooke come downstairs now. Then, when the guys arrive, you take them into the living room and serve the hors d'oeuvres."

"You're having hors d'oeuvres?" Jeri smiled, but her stomach tightened. She didn't want to be in charge. What if she dumped the snacks into Dallas's lap? "What do you want me to serve?"

"Tortilla swirls and Asian meatballs—they're in the fridge." Abby nodded toward a cupboard. "In there are some colored toothpicks. They're for dipping the meatballs in the sweet-and-sour sauce."

"You're making my mouth water!"

"Good." Abby grinned. "Tell that to my home ec teacher. You'll love those swirls. They're tortillas filled with cream cheese and salsa, then rolled up and sliced like little pinwheels." She flattened a canned biscuit, spooned tuna mixture into the center, folded the dough over, and pinched the edges together with a fork. "I'll change clothes while the turnovers bake."

Fifteen minutes later the front doorbell sounded. Jeri checked her reflection in the mirror over the fireplace, took a deep breath, and started down the short hallway.

Rosa came from behind, stepped around her, and opened the door with a flourish. Flashing a bright smile, she ushered the boys in. "Welcome to Hampton House," she said.

Dallas spotted Jeri and grinned. "Hi." He hung his cowboy hat onto the hall tree. Jeri didn't know which was shinier—his polished boots or his silver belt buckle. "You all know Jonathan?" he asked, hooking a thumb at his friend.

Jonathan mumbled "hello." His red tracksuit swished as he tossed his ball cap on one of the hooks.

Rosa stepped between the boys and slipped her arms through theirs. "Let me introduce you to the birthday girl." She led them to the living room, where Emily softly played a song by heart on the piano. "Meet Emily Kirkland," Rosa said.

"Hi, Emily," Dallas said. "Are ya'll having a good birthday today?"

"Yes. Thanks." Emily's smile transformed her plain round face. Dressed in tan Bermudas and a brown shirt, she almost blended into the wood paneling. "That's my roommate, Brooke."

"Hey." Brooke stood framed by the picture window, poised as if waiting to have her photo taken. In her cropped jacket, plaid capris, and sequined flip-flops, she could have been a model. *She must love those capris*, Jeri thought. It looked like she'd outgrown them a while back. Then again, most of Rosa's capris were skin tight, and they were brand new.

Rosa tuned the radio to her favorite music station, and then turned to Jeri. "Wanna get the snacks? I mean, the hors d'oeuvres? Tell Nikki to bring in sodas too." She perched on the arm of the couch beside Dallas, her swinging legs barely covered by her short skirt. "I'll take care of our guests."

"Sure." Jeri turned, wishing now that she *had* borrowed the skirt. Rosa was getting all the attention, and her bossiness was irritating. Who left *her* in charge?

Jeri passed around the hors d'oeuvres, and she was grateful when Brooke offered to help refill people's glasses. Finally Abby came downstairs. "Hi, everybody. I think it's all ready." She headed to the study room. "Follow me. One guy per table, okay?"

"Relax, everybody," the house mother added from the hall where she waited with her camera.

Jeri's heart fluttered. Now what? Would Dallas ask her to sit at his table?

The boys grinned and split up. Rosa, Emily, and Brooke hurried to Dallas's table. Disappointed, Jeri followed Nikki and Abby to Jonathan's table. Very nice, very quiet Jonathan. The boys seated each of the girls before sitting down themselves. Ms. Carter's camera clicked away.

Jeri couldn't remember the last time she'd felt so stiff and awkward. She knew this was all part of Abby's requirement for a good grade, but it felt so silly. She sneaked a glance at Abby, waiting for her to unfold her perfect fan-shaped napkin. Next to her, apparently stumped, Jonathan pondered the three forks by his plate. The formally set table looked odd with plastic silverware, Jeri thought, but cleanup later should be easy.

The seating etiquette seemed pointless to her too. Jeri had to jump back up immediately to help carry in the salads and warm garlic bread sticks. A few minutes later, Jeri whispered, "Abby, sit down and eat." But Abby kept running back and forth to the kitchen, refilling glasses of sweet tea and checking the oven.

Once Emily's glass got knocked over, and Abby jumped up, but Dallas waved her back down. "We've got it," he said, grabbing his napkin. "It's just water."

Conversation felt unnatural and phony until Ms. Carter finished taking photos and left. Then Jeri sensed everyone relaxing. Her own back ached from sitting up so straight, and she slumped in relief. Conversation flowed freely then, although there was a lot more laughing at Dallas's table than theirs.

Jonathan was intent on eating his own meal—two helpings of each dish plus anything the girls couldn't finish. Between bites he asked each girl the same two questions: "Where are you from?" and "Do you have any brothers or sisters?" Jeri shook her head. He must have memorized them from some old etiquette book. Couldn't he dry up so she could hear the conversation at Dallas's table?

Jeri caught snatches of talk about the science fair the following week. She glanced behind her, green with envy at Dallas listening so intently to Emily. She was describing "interactive brain teasers to demonstrate how parts of the brain functioned." Whatever *that* meant!

"She has a good chance of winning," Brooke added. "Ms. Todd said so."

"Impressing the science teacher is one thing," Emily said. "Demonstrating for the judges is something else." She blushed then. "Anyway, Brooke's entry is just as good as mine. She's doing hers on making flowers bloom longer."

Brooke shrugged. "My parents own a florist shop. I grew up watching them arrange flowers."

Jonathan quizzed Abby about her brothers and sisters, drowning out further comments about the science fair. Jeri knew that the winner would walk away with a blue ribbon and a huge scholarship. Abby was competing in it too, with something about the food pyramid.

The month of May was filled with final competitions for scholarships: Abby in the science fair, Rosa's scrapbooking project for the art fair, Nikki's equestrian contest, and the media fair Jeri would compete in. She planned to enter her self-published sixth-grade newspaper.

The newspaper had started as a group assignment early in the school year for herself, Rosa, Abby, and Nikki. It had been an instant hit with their friends—especially Rosa's advice column—so Jeri had decided to keep publishing it. To win at the media fair, all she needed was a zinger of a front-page article. Time was getting short to find something catchy to write about.

Finally Abby stood up. "Ready for birthday cake, Emily?"

"Sure!" Emily was the kind of plain brainy girl you barely noticed, Jeri thought, but tonight she was almost radiant.

"Everybody stay put," Abby said. "I'll be right back."

Jeri pulled the study room's heavy drapes closed to make it really dark, and then she stood by the door. A moment later, Abby called, "Lights out!" Jeri flipped the light switch and then hurried to her seat.

Abby carried in the two-layer birthday cake with twelve blazing candles. Her face shone eerily above the candlelight. "Happy birthday to you!" she sang, and everyone joined in. Dallas laughed when Emily blew too hard on the candles, spraying bits of melted wax across the cake.

Within fifteen minutes the entire cake was gone. Both boys ate two pieces. Emily escaped up to her room with the remaining chunk of cake, saving it for a midnight snack. Then the boys' ride back to Patterson arrived, and Abby walked Dallas and Jonathan to the door, thanking them for their help.

After they left, Abby closed the door and collapsed against it. "I'm bloomin' tired," she said. "Hurray for paper plates."

"I'll help clean up," Jeri said. "You did an awesome job, Abby."

"An *A* is definitely in the bag," Rosa agreed.

Abby and Jeri joked around as they washed and dried the cooking and baking dishes. Nikki and Rosa slumped in the breakfast nook, where Rosa flipped on the portable TV. When Jeri wiped off the table, she was surprised to see Nikki so pale.

"You okay?" she asked.

"Not really." Nikki's skin was an odd shade of green.

Jeri frowned. Actually she was feeling a bit queasy herself.

Standing, Nikki grabbed the edge of the table. "I'm going to bed." She started toward the hallway. "Oh, *man.*" She turned abruptly and stumbled into the small half-bath off the kitchen. She slammed the door shut and threw up, over and over. Jeri's stomach lurched at the retching sounds.

"I'll get Ms. Carter," Rosa said. She raced up the stairs to find the housemother.

Jeri knocked on the closed door. "Nikki, can I help?"

"No," she answered weakly. "I'll be okay."

Jeri looked over her shoulder at Abby. "Are you sick too?"

"No, but I didn't eat that much. Nikki had two big helpings of everything."

Jeri frowned. *I didn't eat that much either.* But if Nikki didn't stop throwing up, the retching threatened to make Jeri vomit too.

Rosa and Ms. Carter rushed into the kitchen. The housemother knocked on the bathroom door. "I'm coming in, Nikki," she said, going in and closing the door.

Jeri, Rosa, and Abby waited in the kitchen. Abby wrung her hands. "Poor Nikki! Do you think there was something wrong with what I cooked?"

"Probably," Rosa said. "Emily and Brooke are sick upstairs too, but not this bad."

Jeri's stomach cramped suddenly. "It's not your fault. Maybe the tuna was old or something. It'll be okay."

It took Nikki forever to stop throwing up. When she finally spoke, her words to the housemother were clear, even through the closed bathroom door.

"Ms. Carter," she moaned, "I think I'm going to die."

faiThGirLz!
the beauty of believing

BOARDING SCHOOL MYSTERIES

A New Series from Faithgirlz!

The Boarding School Mysteries series challenges twelve-year-old Jeri McKane, a sixth grader at the private Landmark School for Girls, to trust God's Word and direction as this amateur sleuth searches for clues in the midst of danger.

Fading Tracks
Softcover • ISBN 9780310714293
On the way home from a field trip, the Landmark School for Girls van, with the driver and six girls, disappears somewhere along the Two-Mile Stretch leading into town. Jeri McKane desperately searches for her missing friends, including her roommate Rosa.

Secrets For Sale
Softcover • ISBN 9780310714309
A blackmailer is victimizing Jeri McKane's best friend, so Jeri uses her investigative abilities to discover who and why. As the threats become more serious—to her friend as well as herself—Jeri dares to confront real danger face-to-face.

Pick Your Poison
Softcover • ISBN 9780310714323
When several girls get sick after a special dinner, everyone assumes the cause is accidental food poisoning. However, after further outbreaks Jeri McKane suspects the poisonings are more sinister.

Available now at your local bookstore! Visit www.faithgirlz.com

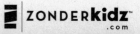

ZONDERkidz
.com

A New Series from Faithgirlz!

Meet Morgan, Amy, Carlie, and Emily. They all live in the trailer park at 622 Harbor View in tiny Boscoe Bay, Oregon. Proximity made them friends, but a desire to make the world a better place—and a willingness to work at it—keeps them together.

Project: Girl Power

Book One • Softcover • ISBN 9780310711865

After a face-off with a group of bullies, Morgan, Amy, Carlie, and Emily decide to walk to and from school together. There's safety in numbers. Then the girls notice how ugly their mobile home park looks. With help from other people in the park, they beautify Harbor View, which brings surprising consequences.

Project: Mystery Bus

Book Two • Softcover • ISBN 9780310711872

The girls of 622 Harbor View begin summer by working to clean and restore their bus to use as a clubhouse. As they work on the bus, they discover clues that suggest someone who lived in the bus during the late '70s had a mysterious past and is somehow connected with grumpy Mr. Greeley, the manager.

Project: Rescue Chelsea

Book Three • Softcover • ISBN 9780310711889

Carlie makes a new friend. Chelsea Landers lives in a mansion and isn't always very kind. Carlie would like a best friend, but will Chelsea fit in with her other friends? When Carlie is betrayed by Chelsea, will she learn to forgive?

Project: Take Charge

Book Four • Softcover • ISBN 9780310711896

The girls of 622 Harbor View find out their town's only city park has been vandalized and may soon be turned into a parking lot. They group together to save their beloved park and soon meet an elderly woman with the power to help their cause, or stop it before it even starts. But will they be able to convince her to help before it's too late?

Project: Raising Faith

Book Five • Softcover • ISBN 9780310713494

When the girls set out to raise the money to go on a three-day ski trip with the church youth group, Morgan is confident that God will provide the funds. But while everyone else finds a way to afford the trip, Morgan's plans are derailed by her grandmother's illness, school, Christmas activities, even jealousy ... and when Grandma suffers a heart attack, Morgan's faith is severely tested. Will God provide what's really important?

Project: Run Away

Book Six • Softcover • ISBN 9780310713500

Shortly before Christmas, Emily's family must flee when her abusive father uncovers them in Boscoe Bay. But Emily's friends rally to help get them safely back home, where Emily discovers that forgiveness doesn't always come easily.

Available now at your local bookstore! Visit www.faithgirlz.com

faiThGirLz!
the beauty of believing

Bibles

Every girl wants to know she's totally unique and special. This Bible says that with Faithgirlz! sparkle! Now girls can grow closer to God as they discover the journey of a lifetime, in their language, for their world.

The NIV Faithgirlz! Bible

Hardcover
ISBN 9780310715818

Softcover
ISBN 9780310715825

The NIV Faithgirlz! Bible

Italian Duo-Tone™
ISBN 9780310715832

The NIV Faithgirlz!
Backpack Bible

Periwinkle Italian Duo-Tone™
ISBN 9780310710127

Available now at your local bookstore! Visit www.faithgirlz.com

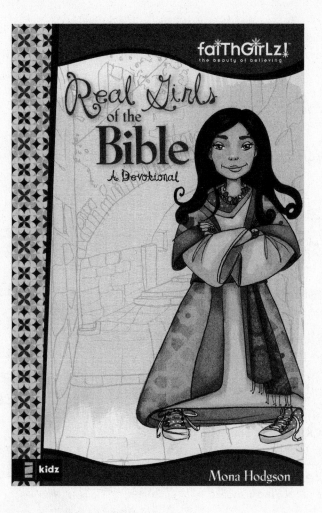

Real Girlz of the Bible: A Devotional

Softcover • ISBN 9780310713388

This devotional includes stories of thirty authentic Bible women to illustrate the power of the girlfriend community to surround and support girls as they become real women of God, while emphasizing each girl's individuality and God's special plan for her.

faiThGirLz!
the beauty of believing

Sophie Series

Meet Sophie LaCroix, a creative soul who's destined to become a great film director someday. But many times, her overactive imagination gets her in trouble!

Sophie's World
Book 1 • Softcover • ISBN 9780310707561

Sophie's Secret
Book 2 • Softcover • ISBN 9780310707578

Sophie and the Scoundrels
Book 3 • Softcover • ISBN 9780310707585

Sophie's Irish Showdown
Book 4 • Softcover • ISBN 9780310707592

Sophie's First Dance?
Book 5 • Softcover • ISBN 9780310707608

Sophie's Stormy Summer
Book 6 • Softcover • ISBN 9780310707615

Sophie Breaks the Code
Book 7 • Softcover • ISBN 9780310710226

Sophie Tracks a Thief
Book 8 • Softcover • ISBN 9780310710233

Sophie Flakes Out
Book 9 • Softcover • ISBN 9780310710240

Sophie Loves Jimmy
Book 10 • Softcover • ISBN 9780310710257

Sophie Loses the Lead
Book 11 • Softcover • ISBN 9780310710264

Sophie's Encore
Book 12 • Softcover • ISBN 9780310710271

Devotions

No Boys Allowed
Devotions for Girls

Softcover • ISBN 9780310707189

This short, ninety-day devotional for girls ages 10 and up is written in an upbeat, lively, funny, and tween-friendly way, incorporating the graphic, fast-moving feel of a teen magazine.

Girlz Rock
Devotions for You

Softcover • ISBN 9780310708995

In this ninety-day devotional, devotions like "Who Am I?" help pave the spiritual walk of life, and the "Girl Talk" feature poses questions that really bring each message home. No matter how bad things get, you can always count on God.

Chick Chat
More Devotions for Girls

Softcover • ISBN 9780310711438

This ninety-day devotional brings the Bible right into your world and offers lots to learn and think about.

Shine On, Girl!
Devotions to Keep You Sparkling

Softcover • ISBN 9780310711445

This ninety-day devotional will "totally" help teen girls connect with God, as well as learn his will for their lives.

Faithgirlz! is based on 2 Corinthians 4:18—So we fix our eyes not on what is seen, but on what is unseen. For what is seen is temporary, but what is unseen is eternal (NIV) — and helps girls find the beauty of believing.

We want to hear from you. Please send your comments about this book to us in care of zreview@zondervan.com. Thank you.